Rebecca Henry is a world traveler. While living in England, Rebecca became inspired by the beautiful countryside and quaint British cottages, collecting inspiration for her writings.

She is also a serious vegan, gardener, crafter, and practises yoga.

Dedication

To my pixie, Penelope and my little man Jude. You are my ever after in this fairy tale of life.

Acknowledgments

To Austin Macauley Publishers for their endless support and belief in my work and a sincere thank you to their design team for the gorgeous cover art.

A warm and heartfelt thank you to my beta reader Fallak Tabassum for her exquisite attention to detail in helping me make *The Lady Raven* what it is.

REBECCA HENRY

THE LADY RAVEN

A Dark Cinderella Tale

AUSTIN MACAULEY PUBLISHERS™

LONDON • CAMBRIDGE • NEW YORK • SHARJAH

A CIP catalog record for this title is available from the British Library.

ISBN 9781786935786 (Paperback)
ISBN 9781786935793 (Hardback)
ISBN 9781786935809 (E-Book)

www.austinmacauley.com

First Published (2017)
Austin Macauley Publishers Ltd.
25 Canada Square
Canary Wharf
London
E14 5LQ

CONTENTS

A Tale of First Tragic Loss

Zezolla was born a princess in the kingdom of Munich. Her father was a devoted one, and he admired his little girl greatly. Zezolla's father would never be king. His older brother, Crown Prince Edwin, was to be the successor of the throne instead. Prince Edwin was loved by all in the land. He had classic good looks, a beautiful wife, and was an expert swordsman, undefeated in battle. In comparison, Prince Baldric was just an average prince. Never truly loved by the King and not particularly talented at anything. He was a 'just in case' prince; a backup in the unthinkable event that anything might happen to the kingdom's hero, Prince Edwin. Although, to Princess Zezolla her father would always be a hero.

Prince Edwin did not love his wife, Princess Annora. She was the daughter of a poor king who ruled a Kingdom that lay off the coast of France. Her true talents lay in her beauty. Princess Annora was widely considered dim-witted, vain, and awfully boring. Her husband was embarrassed by her demeanor.

Princess Annora sat at her mirror, her golden hair falling to the floor. "I want it braided for the feast tonight."

"Yes, Your Highness." Replied her handmaiden, who then carefully separated her hair into three equal sections.

Princess Annora rummaged through her clips, finally selecting a silver vine. "This should do nicely."

"It's beautiful, my princess."

"Yes, it is. My husband spoils me with the most extravagant gifts." She took her eyes off the mirror and glanced at the door just as Prince Edwin threw it open. A trail of servants followed behind, each carrying boxes tied in expensive white satin.

"Love of my life. My night star" sang Prince Edwin. "Why don't you stay inside your chamber this evening and not attend the feast with me. It will be the same drabble attending as in all of the other feasts that have been thrown by my father this past month. Men speaking of their hunts, knights boasting about battle...it would be an unwelcoming and too masculine an event for my delicate, beautiful wife." He placed a kiss upon Annora's head as he stroked her long hair. Princess Annora, who was naive when it came to matters of men, believed that her husband loved her deeply. With each sweet lie he spun, she fell deeper into his web of deceit.

"Oh, my husband! You flatter me so" she fluttered her eyes at her flawless reflection. "Should I really remain in my chamber this evening? Won't the king be displeased if my presence is missing at the feast?" In response Prince Edwin signaled for his servants to bring over one of the decadent boxes.

"I have presents for you, my night star. New gowns imported from France." he said, ignoring her question.

"Gowns? From France!? How many?" Princess Annora jumped to her feet, rushing over to claim her gifts. "Oh! How gorgeous! Look at the shine of this silk, and the beading is exquisite!"

"Wonderful! I'm pleased you like them. Stay in the comfort of your chamber, my love, and enjoy trying on all your new dresses. I will explain to father that you require rest, for I need an heir and too much excitement might overwhelm you and thus prevent you from producing me a son. I will handle the burden of mingling with the rowdy crowd downstairs."

"Yes, I do believe I will stay in, my husband." A servant held one of the expensive gowns against the princess's body. "Prepare my bath, servant. I want to smell like a flower before dressing like one."

Prince Edwin kissed Annora on the forehead before departing from her room. "Until tomorrow, my night star." he said, closing the chamber door.

Prince Edwin sped down the castle hall, wanting to be distanced from his wife. It was eerily quiet in this part of the castle, with everyone at the hall enjoying the feast. Still, he had to be careful that his words were not overheard as he spoke to his trusted attendant. "I cannot stand that sad excuse of a woman" whispered Prince Edwin. "To think my father made me marry her and expects a prince from that half-wit." Prince Edwin resented his father for arranging his marriage. He had wanted to select his own bride, believing that he should have the final say on who the future queen of his kingdom would be.

"Father panicked after my first wife perished during childbirth. Seeing his dead grandson lying in a coffin sent my father into a frenzy. He was unreasonable, ordering me to remarry within the month." The men turned down a corridor leading to a narrow staircase spiraling down to the main level of the castle. "I was able to escape an arranged marriage at that time by going off to Italy to conquer a new land in my father's name. It bought me a few years staying in Italy, but my ultimate mistake was returning home without a bride. Now I'm stuck with this cow." Prince Edwin turned to his attended, and snarled "I wish she was dead."

"I could have her killed, Your Grace."

The prince waved his hand in the air. "No, that won't do. I thought about that, but I do need a son. I will be the king soon and I will need an heir." He took caution whispering his next words. "Although, after my son has arrived, I will have no more need of the beast. I may yet take you up on that offer Jeffery."

"Anything you require, Sire."

Prince Edwin slapped Jeffery on the back. "Now, off to the feast for some women and wine."

"You will soon need other excuses to keep the princess in her chamber, Sire."

Prince Edwin touched his finger to his temple. "We've been husband and wife for six months now. I plan on having the beast pregnant with my son by winter. So far, the woman appears to be barren. If she cannot give me an heir by spring, then I will take a more drastic approach." Prince Edwin sliced his throat with his finger.

Jeffery understood the prince's intentions clearly. "But... if she does manage to conceive a child, then I can order her locked up for the sake and protection of the unborn baby. She will be sent to the childbearing wing to be kept in constant darkness with only the company of nuns to watch over her. No one will be allowed to visit." He smirked, deep into his daydream "even myself."

Prince Edwin's excitement was growing at the thought of locking away his wife. He longed for freedom, as he resented having to pretend to like Princess Annora. Even her voice was a constant annoyance to him, and lying with her was painful as well. He complained of how she required endless compliments even during love making. "After nine months of solitude, she will grow mad and be declared an unfit mother. We will move her to the tower and there you can devise a method of your choice to put the poor princess out of her misery."

"Excellent formula, Your Grace."

"How is my robe, Jeffery? I want to look commanding this evening when entering the great hall."

Jeffery fanned out Prince Edwin's robe, brushing away any wrinkles from the red velvet that draped down to the floor. "Impeccable, Your Grace."

"Good. Let us enter the feast, Jeffery. You may announce me now."

Laughter could be heard from the Great Hall. Knights from all over the kingdom were gathered to participate in a tournament being held at the palace. Wealthy merchants were seated at one of the grand tables. Their chests were covered with expensive clothing and their feet with decadent shoes. Beautiful maidens roamed the feast and Prince Edwin scanned each one as they walked by.

"Not a bad spread tonight, Sire. I'm sure you will find something to suit your fancy."

The prince's eyes searched the hall overlooking the maidens. "I'm not interested in maidens, Jeffery. I've had my share of common women. I'm in the mood for something more prominent." Prince Edwin's gaze landed on his brother. "There's my delicate baby brother." He said, disgusted. "That boy doesn't have a trace of manhood in him. Come, Jeffrey." Prince Edwin strode past the guests, shaking hands and bestowing a quick greeting to all he passed. Everyone bowed and praised the prince as he walked through the Great Hall. The massive candles cast a heavenly glow upon his face. He was indeed extraordinarily handsome and uncommonly charming. It was hard not to adore the prince.

"Baby brother, I see you all alone tonight" said Prince Edwin. "Where is your lovely wife?" Prince Baldric did not enjoy the nightlife of his father's parties. Unlike his elder brother, he was not a sociable man by nature and preferred to spend his evenings quietly in his chamber with his wife, Avelina and daughter, Zezolla.

"Brother," bowed Prince Baldric, "Avelina is in her chamber resting with Zezolla. I, too, would rather be with them, if my presence hadn't been requested by Father to attend the feast."

Prince Baldric took a sip of his wine as he looked around at the drunken strangers before him. "Oh, Brother, you never did like crowds. Always a solo act, you were."

"Yes, well...I'm not solo anymore, dear Edwin. I have my beloved wife and daughter to spend my evenings with and that suits me fine."

"Indeed Brother...Indeed." Edwin raised his glass to Baldric before leaving him alone and at his isolated table.

"Excuse me your Grace, but where, if i may ask, are we going?" Jeffery grabbed a quick glass of wine, chugging it in one gulp as he followed his lord out of the hall.

"I am going to see my love." Edwin stopped, pulling his footman closer. "You, Jeffery, will need to keep that brat away from her mother."

"How am I going to do that, Sire?"

"Bring the brat to her governess."

"Yes, Sire. But Sire, what about your brother? What if he leaves the feast to be with his wife and returns to Princess Avelina's chamber?"

Prince Edwin stroked his chin as he thought. "After sending Zezolla to her governess, you will then inform Princess Avelina's handmaiden to find my brother. Instruct her to tell my brother that Zezolla is with her governess for the evening and Princess Avelina is in bed with a headache and requests that she not be disturbed."

"Of course, Your Grace."

"If there was a more permanent way of separating my brother from his wife, I would use it, but I must play this cautiously a little longer. A great deal depends on the coming months and I cannot put Princess Avelina or myself in jeopardy."

Princess Avelina was sprawled out on her lounge as a handmaiden brushed her hair. Zezolla was sitting beside her mother playing with her glass doll.

"Princess Avelina, you have a visitor" announced her handmaiden.

Princess Avelina raised her head to the servant, completely unsurprised that she would have a caller so late in the evening. "Send him in." Zezolla looked up from her doll and spotted the servant, Jeffery.

"Hello, little Princess, I've been instructed by your father, to take you to the quarters of your governess."

"But my father wanted me to stay here with Mother until he returned from the feast."

"Hush, my sweet." Her mother sat upright helping Zezolla to her feet. "I'm tired, it is late, and I am sure your father will not be back until well after you are asleep. Go with the servant to your governess. I will send for you in the morning, my little love." Princess Avelina kissed her daughter with complete and utter love reflected in her eyes, for Zezolla was her entire heart.

"Come, little Princess. It is time to go." Jeffery turned to Princess Avelina and bowed before exiting her chamber.

Avelina dismissed her handmaiden. "I am tired. Go now for the night. I wish to be alone."

"Yes, My Lady."

Avelina took off her robe, throwing it onto the bed. She pinched her cheeks, adding a touch of color to her lovely, fair face. "All clear my secret lover." She waited patiently for Prince Edwin to enter through the door, her heart beating with excitement. He was not supposed to visit tonight, but she had known that he would. "You can't go one night without seeing me can you Edwin?" She smirked.

Prince Edwin ran to Avelina, throwing her down on the bed. "No, I can't." He kissed her passionately, almost suffocating her with his mouth.

"Edwin! Stop... Stop! We can't go on like this. Someone will see." She playfully pushed Edwin off her.

"It doesn't matter who sees. I'll rip out their tongue so they could never speak of what they saw."

"And what if it is Baldric who sees? If he finds out, he will murder me."

Edwin kissed Avelina's neck, grabbing her hair and pulling it back exposing her bare skin. "Then I'll rip out his eyes so he will never discover us."

Avelina smiled, knowing Prince Edwin's words were not spoken in vain.

Zezolla climbed into her governess's arms. "Wrap up Princess, there's a chill in the air tonight." Zezolla loved being her with governess. She was an attractive and caring woman who always made Zezolla feel loved.

"I wish I could have stayed with Mommy." Zezolla looked up into her governess's eyes. "She is always getting visitors late at night when Daddy is gone."

The governess tilted her head closer to the princess. "What do you mean she's receiving visitors? Is it the same person or many different people paying her visits at night?"

Zezolla shrugged her shoulders. "I never see the face, only the servant…Jeffery. He says Daddy sent him to take me to you." Zezolla brushed the hair from her eyes.

"Little Princess, did you ever ask your daddy why he'd send not his own servant, but his brother's servant, Jeffery, to bring you here?"

"No… Should I?"

The governess smiled an evil smile. "Why yes, Princess. I think your daddy would want to know that you find it curious that Jeffery brings you to see me in the late hours of the night."

Zezolla yawned, feeling the heaviness of sleep. "If you say I should, then I will" said Zezolla while closing her eyes.

"That's a good little princess."

The next morning, the governess waited in her quarters humming the entire time as she rocked in her chair. Her chair faced the ashlars that made up a large portion of her room. She was daydreaming and planning her scheme down to a science. She had known that bringing her mistress, Avelina to the castle would capture the attention of both Princes. All men loved Avelina and she was coveted by all who saw her. The governess had originally planned on Prince Edwin marrying Avelina, but that failed when Prince Edwin had secretly been wed to his first wife in Western Germany. Prince Baldric was the only available option. Another person might have ripped their hair out in distress at plans going awry, but not the governess. Her thoughts operated similarly to that of a master chess player and she always thought multiple steps

18

ahead. She had noticed Prince Edwin eyeing Avelina at his brother's wedding. She was no fool and so she had noticed when he began paying Avelina visits and giving her expensive gifts. Even when Avelina fell pregnant with Zezolla, Edwin had still visited her in the pregnancy wing. "It's almost complete, Lucifer." She whispered to her pet. "It's almost near the end." The governess stroked her cat's fur, both the governess and her cat purring in contentment.

The morning breeze was cold. It was a sign that winter was not too far away and that the leaves had already begun to turn. Zezolla ran through the courtyard as she searched for her mother. She stopped by the Black Oxford Tree and plucked a black apple from a branch. Zezolla sat on the cool ground, tasting the fruit's tantalizing sweetness. The tree had been a gift from the King of Oxford himself, and Zezolla favored this tree above all others in the garden.

"Good morning, sweetheart."

Zezolla looked up. Her father was standing above her. He looked kind and the morning light shined behind him enveloping him with a warm glow.

"Daddy!" She jumped into his arms. "Want a bite? It's delicious."

Her father took a bite of the apple, staring into his daughter's eyes. "You have your mother's eyes, little one. One day, you will grow up to be a beautiful princess just like your mother, and a handsome prince will fall madly in love with you."

"Just like Uncle Edwin did with Mommy?"

Prince Baldric spat out the apple and placed his daughter on the ground. "What? Why would you say such a thing, Zezolla?"

His daughter began to tremble. She had never seen her father so angry. She backed up from him with the realization that she had made a mistake and instantly decided that she would not be telling him any more of what she knew.

"I asked you a question." Prince Baldwin grabbed Zezolla's arm, shaking her as he repeated himself. "Why did you say that?"

"Daddy, I'm sorry. I meant you! I meant to say you."

"Do not lie to me Zezolla."

"Daddy, I'm sorry. Please let me go."

Prince Baldric released his grip, upon realizing that he was tormenting the wrong person. He turned from his daughter and walked, off leaving her alone under the apple tree.

Prince Baldric stormed into his wife's chambers. Princess Avelina sat at her vanity, having already bathed and dressed. "Morning my love, how was the feast last night?" She asked her husband sweetly. Prince Baldric remained calm. Looking at his wife's loving face filled him with disbelief at her betrayal. He grabbed his wife, and embraced her tightly. He started to kiss her as he drew her closer to him... She said something to him, but he did not hear. Thoughts of Edwin in Avelina's bed consumed his every thought.

"Baldric, did you hear me?"

He didn't. He stopped kissing her, glancing at her neck. A small red bite mark bruised her skin. Rage, hatred, and malice arose inside of Baldric. He wanted to snap his wife's neck, feeling her heart stop as he held her. He placed his hands slowly around Avelina's throat, feeling her vein move as her pulse quickened. He began to squeeze ever so slightly. Avelina whimpered. "My love… Your neck is so delicate, so pretty." He whispered in her ear.

Avelina relaxed, exhaling a breath of relief from her husband's unexpected behavior. "Did you sleep at all last night my love? You seem tired."

Baldric looked at his adulterous wife and smiled. "No, dear, I didn't; I really should get some rest, but before I do, come join me for a walk by the lake. I could use the fresh air."

Avelina waved for her servants to follow. "No, love, do not bring your servants this time. Let it be just us. I require absolute privacy."

"As you wish, my love." Avelina dismissed her handmaidens and took her place by her husband's side as they walked to the lake. The indigo water sparkled like a sapphire while elegant swans swam underneath the medieval bridge, and intricate sculptures of gargoyles rested on each end of it, protecting travelers from trolls. "I've always enjoyed it here," sighed Avelina as she scooped up a lily pad from the water.

Prince Baldric walked up behind her. "Zezolla loves the water." Avelina smiled, thinking of her daughter. "One afternoon, she collected an entire basket of lily pads hoping to find a frog prince." She said with a melodic chuckle. Prince Baldric stroked his wife's hair, twisting her long locks around his fingers as if they were his wedding ring.

Avelina giggled. "You haven't played with my hair in years." His grip tightened. "Ouch, Baldric! That hurts!" Baldric yanked on her hair, pulling her neck back. Her face was aimed at the sky. "Baldric! What are you doing? Please stop, it hurts!"

Baldric bent down, whispering into his wife's ear. "I am going to drown you in the river, my love. I want you to hear my words and know that it is I who will kill you. Do not think that I do not know what you did." Before Avelina could protest, her face was plunged into the icy water. She tried pulling her head up, but Baldric was too strong. She began to buck her legs around like a mule, desperate to make contact with Baldric, anything to weaken his grip. Baldric climbed on top of her and pinned her body beneath his. "Die, Avelina." he growled. Hands were flying all around him as he drowned his wife, the only woman he ever loved. Princess Avelina was a fighter and she determined to stay alive, but it was to no avail. Baldric kept her head under the water well after her body stopped moving. Avelina's betrayal caused Baldric's love to turn to hate, just as water turns to ice in the frozen kiss of winter.

"Die, you lying witch. Die! You do not deserve the life you have. You do not deserve me. You have taken everything I've loved away and now I will take everything from you." Baldric's hands trembled with rage as he dismounted his wife's limp body. Baldric arose, looking around the grounds to ensure that no witnesses could testify to his crime. Still, he would not suffer the consequence of murdering his wife. To seal his innocence, he gathered heavy rocks from the bank and shoved them in Avelina's robes.

"They will think it a suicide and my hands will never be traced to her death." He bent down to see her face one last time before kicking her corpse into the lake.

"I loved you mind, body, and soul. I would have loved you until my dying breath, but I will never think of you again. From this day forth, you no longer consume my heart. May you rest in hell, my love." He watched her body sink; he was triumphant, sentencing her to the punishment that fitted the crime: death.

Before her body disappeared into the ultramarine water, he spat on her. One final act of defiance.

From Death Brings Change

Zezolla wore all black to her mother's funeral with her long ginger hair covered in black satin. Zezolla watched as her mother's body descended six feet into the ground. Her father stood by her side, resting his hand on her shoulder. "My sweet little princess, I am sorry you lost your mother."

Zezolla's face was stoic, ice cold like her mother's body. "I do not have a mother now. I only have you, Father." She grabbed his hand, never taking her eyes off the mound of dirt which was now her mother's eternal home.

Prince Baldric bent down, placing Zezolla's hand on his heart. "You will always have me, my sweet little princess. We will survive this terrible loss together." Zezolla's eyes remained locked on the grave. Prince Baldric sensed her need for solitude. "I shall leave you to your thoughts, my tiny love." He kissed his daughter and made his way back to the castle. Day was slowly turning into night, and the sky was bursting with magnificent colors as the dying sun set for her rest.

Zezolla sat by the grave, completely unfazed by the changing night sky. A black raven flew overhead, landing by Avelina's grave. In its mouth was a hazel twig. The bird cautiously made its way closer to the little princess, its black eyes locked on Zezolla's face. "What do you want, raven? Are you here to mock my loss?" The bird came up to the little princess, dropping the twig by her feet. Zezolla picked it up, examining the ordinary branch. "What do you want me to do with this? It's just a silly twig."

The raven bowed his head low, his dark wings extended out. "It is a gift for you, little princess. It is from your mother."

"You can talk?" Zezolla, still numb by grief, had little excitement in her fragile body.

"Yes, little princess. I can."

"Why would my dead mother send me a talking raven with a stick?" She cocked her head to the side as she examined the ordinary twig, turning it over in her tiny hand.

"It is not an ordinary twig, just like I am not an ordinary raven. I was cursed by an evil sorcerer."

"You must be a bad raven to have been cursed."

"I stole from her, little princess. I took a loaf of bread from her cottage to feed my starving sisters. She spared my life but transformed me into a raven, spending the rest of my days stealing food to feed my belly." The raven moved closer to the princess, stopping by her side. "I knew your mother. She would give me ears of corn from the royal garden. I saved her life from a wolf. The beast was hunting your mother as she walked oblivious amongst the grounds. It had been stalking her for days."

"What was my mother doing alone on the castle grounds?"

"She was waiting for a man."

Zezolla's face grew dark. "My uncle."

"Correct, Princess. They had a meeting spot under a hazel tree. Your mother was alone waiting for her lover when the wolf pounced on her. Her cry of horror sent me into action. I swooped down on the beast, plucking its eyes out. It ran away, bloody and blind. Your mother thanked me by supplying me with endless corn and grains from the royal garden. She promised as long as she lived, she would make sure I would never have to steal again. Over time we became friends and she entrusted me with all her secrets. I welcomed the companionship and enjoyed being with your mother. She was an extraordinary woman."

"If you saved her once, why weren't you there to save her again? Why didn't you stop her from drowning?" Zezolla fought back tears which were clouding her eyes.

"Little princess, I could not have stopped it, for I was not there. Your mother sent me on a quest into the forest in search of a rare root."

Zezolla rubbed her tired eyes, too overcome by emotions to follow the raven's words. "A root? I don't understand why my mother would require a root."

"Princess… Think back. I know you are young, but you must try to remember your mother's actions. Wasn't it she who treated your illnesses and not the royal physician?" Zezolla thought about the time her mother sent servants into the forest for mug wort when she fell from a tree and badly cut her leg, her flesh torn open, exposing the muscle. She closed her eyes, remembering her mother's words as she spread the herb onto her flesh.

"Don't worry, my little love. A bit of mug wort with a touch of a mother's magic will heal you." In the morning, to the princess's amazement, her leg was fully healed and only a tiny scar remained. Zezolla lifted her dress, rubbing her finger over the scar.

"Yes. Mother had her private ways of healing me."

"She always healed you. Do you recall falling ill with the fever and your father sent for all the great healers in the land to save you?"

Zezolla looked at the talking raven, amazed by all he knew. "I do. She somehow found a rare herb called Astragalus. I don't know where she got it from, but she made me a tonic from the herb and the fever departed."

"Little princess, it was I who retrieved the herb for your mother." He bowed once more, showing his devotion to the princess.

"Then it is I who should be bowing to you, black raven, for I owe you my life." Zezolla bowed her head to the bird.

"Princess… Let me ask you one more question, if I may." Zezolla nodded "yes" at her new companion. "Did you ever wonder why all men adored your mother, particularly your uncle?"

"I assumed it was because of her beauty, raven."

"Ahhh…Yes. She was beautiful, but that was not the reason why men such as your uncle coveted her. Unsatisfied with the marriage to your father, Princess

Avelina decided to make Prince Edwin fall in love with her. She conjured a powerful spell used from the leaves of Ashwagandhas. The leaves of this plant are known as Withanolides. Once ingested, it releases an aphrodisiac effect. Your mother began to give Prince Edwin a tonic made from the herb's leaves. Avelina's beauty and charm was just the lure for her prey, but it was the tonic which snared her victims into a lustful desire.

Your uncle was hooked immediately. He became obsessed with Avelina and the feeling of ecstasy which came upon him whenever he was with your mother. Her strategy was a simple one. Prince Edwin would grow mad in his desire for Avelina, leading to the murder of both his wife and your father. Princess Avelina would marry Prince Edwin, ensuring you to be next on the throne. Once married, Avelina would use yet another tonic, Belladonna, or otherwise known as deadly nightshade, to poison your uncle, leaving your mother Queen of Munich, and you, my little princess, the future queen."

Zezolla stared emotionless at the raven, listening to the true nature of her beloved mother. "Mother was a witch?" she asked cautiously.

"Neither a bad witch nor a good witch – she was just a witch using the ancient methods of the earth for her worldly desires."

"But she wanted to leave my father which would have resulted in his death. How could my mother have such grave intentions?"

"Your father is not the man he appears to be. Your mother slowly discovered that. She was able to see deep within human hearts and deep into their souls. What she saw in your father was evil. Your mother's intentions have only been for you. You were all that mattered to her."

"And now she is dead…" Whispered Zezolla.

"Yes, Princess, but not gone. Her spirit summoned me the moment of her death. I found her before the guards discovered her dead body. She told me her death was not suicide, but murder."

"Murder?" Zezolla extended her arm so the raven would perch upon it. "But who would want to murder my mother?"

"Think, little princess, who indeed? Who would want to cast your mother into the icy cold waters, drowning her as she struggled for life?"

"Was it my uncle, raven?"

"Your uncle's heart is dark, my little princess. His appetite is greedy, and I dare say he will not make a just king. Your mother feared for the kingdom with Prince Edwin in power. But alas, little princess, he is not the murderer I speak of."

"No! I know what you are going to say and it's not possible. My father loved my mother. He would never kill her." The little princess shook her head as tears began staining her cheeks.

"A man so in love with his wife that when he discovered her secret affair with his older brother, he snapped in a moment of rage and jealousy, murdering his true love."

"No!" Zezolla threw her body over her mother's grave, unable to stop the tears which poured from her soul. "It's not possible."

"Oh, but it is, sweet princess, and your mother wanted me to inform you of the true story of her death."

Zezolla laid on the fresh dirt, feeling the earth shift underneath her as if her mother was reaching for her little girl from beneath the earth's crust. "What am I supposed to do, raven, now that I know this horrid truth?"

"The branch, Princess. As I said, it is a gift from your mother. You will be moving soon. An event I cannot divulge any further information in, but when you do, you will be away from your mother's grave and unable to visit her. In time you will plant this hazel branch in the garden of your new home and a magical tree will grow. Your mother's spirit will come to the tree, living inside. There she will be able to communicate with you in words and in other ways."

The princess picked up the hazel branch, pressing it up against her chest, her breaths falling in sync with the beating of her heart. "Will you be there? Will you stay with me?"

"Always, Princess. As long as you love me, treat me as your own, and never allow me to go hungry or in need of stealing, I will always be your faithful companion as I was to your mother."

Prince Edwin was overcome by grief at the loss of Avelina. He stayed inside his chamber, only venturing out at night to visit his lover's grave. His hate for his wife grew steadily stronger as he secretly wished it was her who lay dead in the grave and not Avelina. Prince Baldric kept a watchful eye on his brother, enjoying the torment he had caused him. As Prince Edwin stayed locked in his room, Prince Baldric took company from Princess Annora. The princess, being starved of attention, welcomed Baldric's visits. Her shallow heart was not concerned for the grief which caused her husband such dismay; her only focus was on the affections Prince Baldric bestowed upon her. She relished in pure vanity, adoring Baldric's praises and lovely gifts. Prince Baldric rested in Annora's lap spinning lies of how blessed he would be to have a wife such as her.

Prince Baldric sent musicians to Annora's chamber composing songs of her endless beauty. In the garden by Avelina's grave, Baldric had a statue carved from granite depicting Annora's timeless face. Neglected by her husband, Princess Annora welcomed each act of seduction from Prince Baldric. In return, she gave herself, mind, body, and soul, to her husband's brother. "I owe you my gratitude for all your attention and gorgeous gifts, Baldric." She walked over to Baldric as he sat on her bed. As the room glowed by firelight, Annora stood before him, completely naked. "I want to thank you." She placed his hands on her waist. "My gift to you, Baldric, is my body."

Baldric brought Annora's body into his, wrapping his arms around her. He traced his fingers along her bare back. "I gladly accept such a generous gift from such a beautiful princess."

Baldric visited Annora every evening, neglecting his daughter. As Baldric grew closer to Annora, Zezolla was forced to spend her days in the company of her governess. "Daddy is in love with Princess Annora."

The governess looked down at the little princess, hugging her knees to her chest. "What makes you think that, Princess?"

"He spends all his nights in her chamber, and he sleeps all day. He never visits me." Zezolla rocked back and forth on the stone floor. "Ah, little princess, a man's body is not meant to be without another's. He is seeking comfort the only way he knows how, Princess. It is not love, I assure you." The governess looked down at her sewing, feeling content with the progress.

"I don't understand. To me, it looks like he has given his heart to Princess Annora."

"How does that make you feel little princess?"

"Angry."

"Angry? Don't you mean jealous, sweet child?" Lucifer sat on the governess's lap, purring his evil purr.

"No. I mean anger. He does not deserve love, not for what he did."

A smiled flickered across the governess's face. "I see. Well then, my sweet little princess, you should prevent your father from having his happiness."

"How?"

"By taking away the one thing that brings him joy."

Zezolla looked out the window, her black raven perched on the sill looking back at her.

That evening Zezolla waited for her raven. "I need your help, raven. I have kept up my end of our bargain and I need something from you." Zezolla spoke to her bird as the moonlight guided her to her mother's grave.

"Anything, little princess."

"It is cold tonight, my raven. I can feel my mother's spirit growing restless." Zezolla sat upon her mother's grave, staring intensely at the night sky. She wrapped her arms around her chest for warmth. "I need a tonic that will make Princess Annora pregnant with a babe."

The raven moved onto the grave, resting beside the tiny girl. "You want Princess Annora to become pregnant with your father's child?"

"Yes."

"But why, little princess? Your father does not deserve happiness."

"My governess wants me to take away my father's joy, but I have seen enough sadness, raven. I do not wish anymore pain. I would like something good to come from the sorrow. If my uncle is unfit to be king, then his seed should not produce a lineage. Let this pregnancy be a new birth for our kingdom."

The raven listened for his dead mistress's spirit, waiting for guidance. "As you wish, my little princess. Your mother agrees." Zezolla held out her arm for the raven. She was tired and cold. The night air only held pain and despair for the tiny princess. She would receive no comfort from a grave.

Zezolla sat alone in the stillness of her room. Days passed, turning sunlight into darkness, a continuous rhythm of beginning and ending. Zezolla had little patience for the royals in the castle. No one knew her suffering. No one understood the loss she carried. Her father was a murderer and her mother had forever departed from this life. All Zezolla knew was heartache. Seven days later, the raven returned with herbs tied in a sack upon his back. "I have done what you asked, little princess."

"Then it is time, my raven."

"Follow me, little princess, and I shall take you to the same hazel tree where your mother used to venture." The raven led Zezolla through the castle grounds, and they came to the edge of the garden. A line of majestic trees created a barrier, separating the castle grounds from the forest. A single hazel tree sat amongst a sea of elms. The raven touched the hazel tree with his beak and an opening emerged, allowing access inside the tree. The princess did not ask questions as she ventured inside, her raven guiding her. A winding staircase made from massive roots descended down into the earth. Zezolla made her way deeper inside the hazel tree, counting the steps as she clambered to the top.

"Twenty…twenty-one…twenty-two…. How deep will we venture, my raven?" The raven flapped his wings, awakening the candles which lined the altar. Zezolla made her way to the bottom of the staircase. Black candles sat on the tree's natural shelves.

"This is where your mother preformed her rituals, little princess." Skulls of small animals lined the altar. Jars of insects, sachets of herbs and tails of rats rested on a narrow table inside the center of the tree. Zezolla took off her hood and examined the sight before her. "What am I to do?"

The raven untied the satchel from his back, handing her the herbs. "Take the herbs and mix them in one of the mortars there."

Zezolla did as she was instructed, placing the contents into a mortar and crushing them into a fine powder.

"Now, princess, spit into it."

Again, she did as she was told, mixing the ingredient into the herbs.

"Place the powder into one of those vials, princess."

Zezolla grabbed a small vial from a nearby shelf and carefully filled it with the herbs.

"One last step before it is complete. You must take a pinch of earth from your mother's grave and add it to the vial." Zezolla did as she was told and mechanically made her way back down the stairs and out into the night sky. She walked up to her mother's grave with the black raven resting on her arm. Slowly, she bent down, obtaining a tiny pinch of earth.

"Now, repeat after me, princess." The raven flew up to Zezolla's shoulder, speaking in her ear. "Take my gift and make it grow. Sow the seeds of a prince, bringing life to a king, the heir to the throne."

Zezolla worked the spell, concentrating on the words as she spoke them. A tiny tornado formed inside the vial. "How do we make sure Princess Annora drinks it, raven? I am not allowed into her chambers when my father visits her."

The raven took the vial from Zezolla's hand and clutched it in his claw. "That, little princess, is a task I shall complete." He flew off into the black sky, leaving Zezolla alone, death and darkness her only companions.

Princess Annora knew it the moment she conceived. She felt the unborn baby stir inside her. She looked over at Baldric, sleeping obliviously in her bed. A lovely black raven flew to her window. Annora took it as a sign of her conception. "Lovely bird, are you here to tell me I am cursed for sleeping with my husband's brother? I know I am pregnant. Will the baby be born a monster?"

The raven flew into the room, resting beside the princess. "No, my fair princess, you are not cursed, but blessed. The child you carry will be a boy and will be the heir to the throne. Your king will soon fall ill, and Edwin will be named the new King of Munich."

"But it is not his child! I am pregnant with Prince Baldric's baby. Once Prince Edwin finds out, he will have me beheaded." Princess Annora exclaim, fear evident in her eyes. She sat up in horror at the fate awaiting her.

"Calm yourself, my fair princess. I can help."

"How? What can you do?"

"You must go to your husband's chamber and lay with him."

"He never sleeps with me. I haven't seen him in weeks."

"He will sleep with you tonight."

"How?" she asked in disbelief.

"I have taken care of it, just as I have taken care of your conception. All you have to do is walk into his chamber."

Princess Annora wrapped a robe around her naked body and followed the raven down the narrow passage of the castle. A secret entrance took the princess directly to Edwin's chamber. He lay drunk and alone in his bed. The raven blew out the candles with his wings and instructed Annora to lie beside her sleeping husband.

"Edwin... Edwin. My love, it is I, your Avelina." The raven's voice filled Edwin's ears with the sound of his dead lover.

"Avelina... My true love. You have come back to me."

"Yes, my love. I have." Replied the raven.

Annora, seeing her opportunity, began to kiss her husband. Edwin, overrun by yearning, passionately made love to his wife, believing it was the ghost of Avelina. The raven stayed close by, waiting for the act to be completed. Annora was thankful for the deception and welcomed her husband's embrace, relieved that both her life and her unborn child's life were now safe and secure.

The morning light streaked through the prince's chamber, awakening him from his drunken state. He looked down at the naked woman wrapped in his arms and threw her body to the ground in disgust. "You! How did you get in here? My guards were outside the door." he growled in disgust by his wife's appearance.

Annora was victorious in her mission and arose calmly, wrapping her robe around her. "You have given me the child I have been required to have by the orders of your father, the king. The heir is now secure. You needn't lay with me ever again, husband." Edwin watched in anger as his wife exited through the secret entrance on which she came.

Months passed and word spread of the princess's condition. She was not kept in the pregnancy wing. Instead, she remained in her chamber, pampered by the king's personal servants. Edwin grew deeper into his dark state, cursing his wife for her act of treachery. He did not want a son. He did not want his wife to be Queen of Munich, mother to the future king.

Seasons passed and the princess thrived in her pregnancy. The unborn baby grew strong in her womb. On the eve of her delivery, the king spontaneously fell ill. The royal physician's speculated it was due to rotten meat. The king had been terribly unwell, violently throwing up his insides; blood came pouring out from his mouth like rain.

"He will not live through the night to see the birth of his grandson," the physician informed Prince Baldric.

Prince Baldric sent for his brother to come to his father's side. "He will die within the hour, Edwin, and you will be named king."

Edwin stared down at his dying father and felt no remorse. "Let him die. He's had his reign." He spat callously.

Baldric stood up, cursing his brother for his coldness and the black heart which beat inside him. "You are ugly, brother."

"I am ugly and spiteful." Agreed Prince Edwin. "I am filled with hate and malice. I do not care if Father dies and I do not care if my wife dies along with the beast she's about to deliver." He turned to face Baldric. "I do not care if you die, brother. All I ever cared about has already perished from this life. I care only for myself. I will be named king and you will be sent away to marry another in Southern Germany. You are forbidden to return. This land is no longer your home."

Their father, the king, took a final breath as he sat up, looking into his first born's face. The son who would be king. "Die, father... Your time is over." Edwin's words were vengeful and filled with power. The king did as his son commanded; his heart stopping as he looked into the eyes of his murderer – his first born. Edwin grabbed his brother by the back of his head. "It has all been arranged, brother. You will leave tonight. Pack up your little princess and be gone. I never want to see your face again. If you disobey me, I will take care of you as I did our father."

A carriage awaited Prince Baldric and his daughter. They were to arrive in Southern Germany in two days' time. Zezolla clung to her governess as she walked to her mother's grave. Zezolla grabbed a handful of earth and placed it in her coat pocket. She had her twig, her last gift of her mother clutched in her right hand. "I'm ready governess. Take me to the carriage. I never want to return to this awful place ever again." Zezolla looked to the sky, her loyal raven flying above. She extended the branch, calling him down. "Stay with me, raven. Follow close behind. Don't leave me alone in this world."

"As you wish, my little princess."

The queen gave birth to a strong baby boy in the early hours of the morning whom she named Ferdinand. Delighted with her little prince, she commanded all wet nurses to leave her alone with the babe. She would be the only woman to feed her beloved baby. King Edwin never visited his queen or his son. He despised the infant and he had many failed attempts at killing the baby. His queen was clever; more so than he gave her credit for. She would not allow anyone to feed her son or herself. She took her meals alone in her chamber and she would not allow her son out of her sight, not even for a second.

The queen formed allies of her own. Rebels who did not want the murderous king to reign. Many concluded that Edwin was the culprit behind the king's untimely demise. Edwin's arrogance blinded him from assessing the loyalty of the kingdom. He was unaware that a rebel force was growing against him. The little prince was beloved by all and Queen Annora was idealized for the kindness she bestowed amongst the poor. Becoming a mother had transformed Annora from a somewhat shallow princess into a devoted queen. Queen Annora used her new position to make her kingdom a better place for her little prince. She knew it was only a matter of time before the rebels attempted to assassinate King Edwin, and she would die before she ever allowed Munich to fall into poverty for when her son became king to the throne.

One evening, the queen was visited by an unexpected friend. The raven landed on the queen's window ledge. "My darling blackbird. I didn't know if I would ever see you again." The baby prince lay sleeping in his cradle. The raven bowed to the queen, asking permission to enter her chamber. "Come in, my friend. I owe you my son's life and the fate of his future."

"It was my pleasure, Your Majesty. But I have come to inform you that whispers are in the air. Tonight will be the night your husband will die."

The queen, unfazed by the news, looked down at her baby. "Now would be an opportune time for it. My son is a year old this very evening. He is growing strong and he is already greatly adored by the kingdom." She walked over to her vanity, glancing at her reflection. "I will be able to maintain the kingdom until my son is ready to rule." The queen smiled at her little friend as he perched on the window sill. "How will it happen? Do I have time to pay him a visit first?"

"It has already begun, my queen."

A murderous scream pierced the air, breaking the silence. Servants were outside the halls running in terror. "The king has fallen. To the king, to the king!"

The queen cocked her head. "Poison, my little friend?" Asked Annora.

"No, my queen."

"Hmm… Perhaps a fatal stabbing?"

"Guess again, my queen."

"Really? I'm not sure, then. Please, tell me how my dear husband met his death."

"He is not dead. Not yet, my queen. You still have time to say your goodbyes." The raven bowed before flying out the window, leaving the queen alone with her son.

"Come, my little prince." She lifted her son from his cradle. "It is time to say our farewells to the king." The queen entered her husband's chamber through the same passage she took when she laid with him. He moaned in his bed, an arrow through his chest. His breathing was shallow; his robes stained in blood.

"He does not have long, my queen. A moment or two at best." Said the guard as she approached her husband's bed.

"Guards, leave us. I require privacy with my husband." The queen sauntered over to the dying king, her baby safely cradled in her arms. "You see this man, my little prince? This man is not your father." The king's eyes flashed open, hatred stirring in them. "Yes. This is not your son, my pathetic love. This baby whom I hold before you will be ruler of this land. He will be an honest, good king, and loved by all. His legacy will be one recorded throughout history as a reign of peace and prosperity. I will make sure your name is erased and never to be spoken of."

She bent down, kneeling beside the king's dying form. She watched the life fleet from his body with hungry eyes. "I knew you were having an affair with Avelina; I always knew. I was not as foolish as you thought. I was just biding my time for a son, but your weak, pathetic body could never impregnate a woman. You were not man enough to give me or your lover a seed. So I accepted the seed of another. A man who could create a baby with me."

42

She took her hand, placing it at the head of the arrow. "Your brother." She jammed the arrow deeper into his chest, never breaking eye contact with the man who once broke her heart.

A Stepmother for a Princess

Zezolla adored her new home at Hinterhohen Castle. It was quaint and gothic, unlike the castle in Munich, which she found to be massive and overwhelming. Zezolla felt oddly at peace in the quiet castle. Her father had married Princess Guinevere in a private ceremony. Her new stepmother would never be queen. Princess Guinevere's older brother sat on the throne; a young and accomplished king who would rule throughout his sister's lifetime. He resided in the majestic Neuschwanstein Castle, which rested amongst the white-tipped mountains of the Bavarian Alps. The castle sat 2,620 feet in the sky and presided grandly above Hinterhohen and the mystical village of Gorham. Zezolla's stepmother desperately wanted to be queen and to rule over the kingdom. In order to appease his greedy sister, the King constructed a smaller castle one thousand feet below his own. He honored his sister's marriage to Prince Baldric by giving them servants and livestock. Prince Baldric was content. He had found a young bride, a beautiful castle, and wealth.

Because of these things, Zezolla never saw much of her father. Her new stepmother was needy, requiring all of Prince Baldric's time and attention. Zezolla found companionship amongst the livestock instead, as she preferred the company of animals to people. After discovering the truth of her murderous father, Zezolla had lost faith in human goodness.

The servants feared Zezolla, calling her Hexe, which was German for witch. Rumors of the little princess went around amongst the servants. They would whisper to each other, "its Hexe", as Zezolla roamed the castle halls at night, dressed in black with her raven perched on her shoulder. "Here comes Hexe. Don't look her in the eye. If you do, she will hex you."

"They think I'm a witch, raven." Zezolla toured through the castle halls, the moonlight following behind her.

"Maybe you are, my little princess."

Zezolla glanced at her beloved raven. "Maybe…" She trailed off. Zezolla wandered into the courtyard, barefoot, perching her tiny body on the root of a large beech tree. The castle glowed in the darkness, warm and inviting. Zezolla fixed her eyes on her stepmother's chamber. "Look at her, raven. She's a disgrace to all females. Look at how she controls my father, making him comb her hair and dress her. She has servants for that." Zezolla's sharp gaze sent a shiver to Guinevere's graceless form, penetrating through the ashlar to her stepmother.

Guinevere knew Hexe was watching and an ominous feeling came over her. She peered out the window and saw Zezolla staring back at her. "Your wretched daughter is spying on us again, Baldric. Look! Down there, she wanders the grounds at night." Guinevere shoved her husband toward the window, her temper rising. "You need to speak to Zezolla about her bizarre behavior. The servants are scared of her."

Baldric looked down at his frail daughter, the moonlight shining upon her delicate face. "She's just a child, my love. She's still mourning the death of her mother. Give her time." Guinevere turned away from her husband in disgust, placing distance between them.

"Will you always defend that girl? I am your wife! If I say she is bothersome, then it is your duty as my husband to make her stop. I don't like being spied on." Guinevere sulked, folding her arms over her chest as she glared at the coward before her.

Baldric sighed. He had no desire to upset his wife. "I will speak with her, my love."

"See that you do, my husband, for if you do not, I will ship your precious daughter to Finland to marry the Ice Prince." Guinevere laughed. "Wouldn't that be fitting?"

"Not at all, my love. Please do not do that to Zezolla. I will talk to her. I promise."

"I don't like children, Baldric. I've never wanted to be a mother." She started toward Baldric, gently stroking his hair with her tender fingertips. Her tone softened. "If you think I will bear you children and be a loving mother to Zezolla, you, my dear husband, are mistaken. Make her stop her witchy ways or I will send her off to the coldest part of the world and you will never see your beloved little princess again."

Baldric, knowing he was defeated, promised his wife he would take control of his mourning daughter. "You will see a change in her, my love. I will make sure of it."

Guinevere raised an eyebrow. "You'd better, husband, or I will do it myself. Two years is more than enough time to recover from grief. I have been patient with her horrid ways, and I will not tolerate this behavior any longer."

Zezolla sat below the branches of the massive tree, caressing the moss which grew around her; embraced her, almost. "I wonder what my stepmother is planning. I know she despises me. Good thing I have my raven to be my eyes and ears." The raven circled the moon as he flew down to his little princess, landing softly beside her. "What did you see, my raven?"

"Your stepmother controls your father, Princess. He is completely under her power."

Zezolla nodded. "What did you hear, my raven?"

"Your stepmother plans to get rid of you by sending you off to Finland to marry the Ice Prince."

Zezolla's cobalt eyes glowed in the night sky as if they were tiny shards of the moon itself, reflecting its supernatural luster. "Does she now?" She stroked her raven's shiny black feathers. "And what of my father? Did he agree to this arrangement?"

"Yes, my princess. If he cannot convince you to stop roaming the grounds at night, stop your mourning, and your bizarre behavior, your stepmother will send you away without a moment's notice."

Zezolla took out a ball of dark chocolate from her pocket and offered it to her loyal friend. "Then we will have to devise a plan, my beautiful raven."

On their walk back to the castle, Zezolla heard a cry. Not a human cry, but an animal in distress. "Raven, do you hear that?" The raven flew off into the darkness, blending in with the sky as Zezolla trailed close behind him.

"Little princess, it sounds as if there is a mouse in trouble."

Zezolla crawled on her hands and knees, following the fragile cry. The sound led to a small hole embedded in the garden's large stony walls. Zezolla peeked inside the hole and two tiny red eyes glared back. "You are correct, my raven. It is a mouse." Zezolla put her hand inside the hole. "Come out, little one. I will not harm you." The little mouse hopped onto Zezolla's hand. "You are covered in blood, little one, but I do not see any wounds. Is this not your blood?" It was just then that Zezolla saw the owl coming towards her. The raven flew above Zezolla's head, spreading its enormous wings, protecting Zezolla. She ducked, clenching the mouse within her fists.

"Away with you, owl, or I will pluck out your eyes!" Cried the raven. The owl screeched a terrifying screech as it darted at Zezolla, not heeding the raven's warning. "Away with you!" Repeated the raven.

The raven lunged for the owl as it circled the little princess. "He wants the mouse, Princess," whispered the raven.

Zezolla felt the tiny creature trembling in her hand. "He cannot have it, raven! Pluck out his eyes!" The raven obeyed his little princess and charged at the owl. Then they took off, flying higher and higher into the clouds as they fought. Screams surrounded the princess as she laid on the ground. "Raven. Raven!" Zezolla exclaimed, frightened for her raven's life. Her eyes danced over toward to the black sky, hoping to spot her lovely raven. "Raven! Please, come back to me!" And as if on cue, her faithful companion swooped down, landing beside the princess's face. Blood stained the raven's beak. "Oh, my sweet raven! I thought you were dead!"

The raven bowed. "Never, my little princess. I will never depart from you in this world."

Zezolla opened her hand, releasing the petrified mouse, meek and frozen with fear. "Off you go. The owl is gone. You can return home."

The mouse scurried inside the hole, returning with a dead baby in its paws. "Oh my, the owl was feasting on your young?" Zezolla's heart broke. She gently picked up the dead baby. "Are there more, little mouse?" Again, the mouse returned from the hole, carrying two more dead babies. "I will bury them, little mouse, so you may visit their grave." Zezolla used her hands to dig into the earth. She took off the black satin which hung in her hair. Carefully, she wrapped the little mice in the satin, placing them in the ground.

"I am sorry for your loss, little mouse." The mouse bowed, showing his gratitude, then scampered back into the hole seeking, solitude and shelter from the merciless world around him. "Come, my raven. I have seen enough death and loss for one night." Zezolla wrapped her arms around her frail body, wishing her mother was there to comfort her. Zezolla went to her governess, seeking a mother's love, even if it was not her own. After all, in a situation such as this, anything would do.

"My little princess, you have blood on your hands. Are you hurt?" Zezolla fell into her governess's arms, wanting to feel the warmth of a woman. "No, Governess, I am not." Lucifer jumped on Zezolla's lap, licking the blood from her hands.

"What troubles you, my little princess? Your face is grave tonight." She stroked the little princess's face, offering comfort.

"My father is to send me away by the orders of Princess Guinevere."

The governess cupped Zezolla's face. "Why?"

"Because she finds me bothersome and odd. She wants me not to be seen nor heard. She says she doesn't like children."

The governess glanced at her cat, realizing her plans were in jeopardy. "My sweet little princess, I can't imagine anyone could ever not love nor want you. Why, if I were your stepmother, I would treat you as if you were my own." She embraced the princess, retaining eye contact with Lucifer.

"Oh, if only you were my stepmother, Governess. Then I could finally be happy. I do not have a mother or a father. You are all I have."

The governess smiled as she groomed Zezolla's hair with her long, spindly, witch-like fingers. "There is a way, my little princess."

"I'll do anything."

"If Guinevere was gone, your father would be a free man." The governess paused. "I could marry your father and you would never be alone again."

"But that's impossible! Only death can separate what has been joined in marriage."

The governess whispered into the princess's ear, a secret meant solely for them. Lucifer circled his mistress's heels, listening to the future events about to take place. The governess did not sleep that night. She stayed in her rocker, staring at the wall with her cat curled up in her lap. "This is not the event I planned for, my handsome Lucifer, but this may be an even better strategy working to our benefit." Lucifer purred, kneading the governess's thighs with his paws. "If Zezolla follows my instructions and sticks to the plan, this could be the ultimate outcome for us, my love. Yes... We will have it all." She looked down at her cat. "Just make sure she doesn't lose her nerve when the time comes. I will need you there, my love. If she hesitates, you must finish it and do whatever it takes." Lucifer licked her hand, showing his devotion to his mistress. "That's a good Lucifer."

Prince Baldric visited his daughter for the first time in weeks. His servants brought an iron chest filled with gowns for the little princess. "Hello, my darling. I have a gift for you."

Zezolla sat in her chair, never standing to greet her father. "Thank you, Father, you may place it there." She pointed to the center of the room. The servants cautiously entered Zezolla's chamber, keeping their eyes off the little princess dressed in black.

"My little princess. I have brought you new gowns in hopes of retiring your black ones." Zezolla flashed her father a murderous look. "And what is wrong with my black gowns?"

Prince Baldric turned to his servants. "Leave us." He warned, walking over to his daughter. "Sweet love, your mother has been dead and buried almost two years now. It is time to stop your mourning and rejoin the world of the living."

Zezolla glared. Hatred arose inside her. "I am not ready."

"Zezolla… You will never be ready unless you try. You are upsetting your poor stepmother. How can she love you when you are always in mourning?" He turned around the room. "Look at this chamber! It is a coffin for death." He began ripping down tapestries, throwing the bedspread on the floor. He opened her wardrobe and ripped her black dresses in half. "Black! Black! Everything in here is black!" He whirled around, staring the raven dead in the eye. "And this creature! Who keeps a raven for a pet? It is not sane, Zezolla. It is not normal! I command you to stop this behavior this instant." Zezolla remained seated in her chair, unfazed by her father's sudden outburst. "Are you deaf, child? Did you not hear me?"

"I am not deaf, Father. I did hear you." Her calmness drove Prince Baldric to rage.

He grabbed the princess's glass doll, a present from her mother at birth. "I'm warning you, Zezolla, you must stop this behavior."

"What behavior is that, Father?"

Baldric threw the doll against the stone wall, shattering Zezolla's heart for the final time. Her eyes screamed in pain, her lips quivered with hate, yet she remained silent, her stoic look returning to her face.

"Don't play dumb with me, girl! The servants are talking about you! They see you roaming around at night, speaking to mice, and burying their young in the earth!" He turned on her now, grabbing the sides of her chair. "What princess behaves in such a manner? How can your stepmother love you, or even like you, when you are acting like a Hexe!"

Zezolla's nostrils flared. She glanced at her raven for guidance. He nodded encouragingly for her to continue with the next phase of the plan. "Perhaps, Father, if my stepmother came to me and helped me don these new gowns, I might feel more inclined to be a perfect princess again."

Baldric released his grip from the chair. He backed away, giving space between him and his daughter. "You would stop this ridiculous behavior if your stepmother were to come to you?" Zezolla nodded yes; her eyes softening. "You truly just want a mother again, don't you, my little princess?" Again, Zezolla nodded. "Then I will send for her."

Zezolla remained in her chair, patiently waiting for her stepmother's arrival. "You cannot be here, my raven, when my stepmother enters. She will be turned off by your presence."

"I understand, my little princess."

"I do not wish to be alone, though, my raven."

"I will send for Lucifer to stay with you."

Zezolla looked lovingly at her black bird. "I do love you so, raven."

"And I love you, my little princess… Always."

Lucifer entered through the passage connecting Zezolla's room and her governess's. "Hello, cat. Please stay with me while my stepmother is here. I'm afraid I'll lose my nerve." Zezolla looked at her hands as they folded neatly into her lap like napkins on a table, wondering if she had the courage to play out the plan her governess had instructed for her. Lucifer jumped on the edge of her bed, purring an evil purr. Zezolla heard her stepmother approaching the door. "She's here, Lucifer."

Guinevere entered Zezolla's chamber with her handmaidens following behind her. "Little princess, your father said you wished for my company," said Guinevere, annoyed. She twirled around the wrecked room, disgusted by the macabre scene before her. "Clean this up." She snapped her fingers to her servants.

"Please, Stepmother… May they do that later? I was hoping for time alone with you, just us."

Guinevere snarled at the little princess. "Why would we do that?"

"Because, Stepmother, I want to please you. I want to come out of my mourning and wear those beautiful gowns Father has brought me, but I can only do that in the privacy of your company." Guinevere sighed, staring down at the trunk. "Very well, Princess. Be gone now, servants. I'll summon you later to clean up this dreadful room."

"Thank you, Stepmother."

Guinevere waved a hand in the air, dismissing the princess's gratitude. "Cats... You now have cats as well."

"No, Stepmother. He belongs to my governess."

"I am not fond of cats, or ravens, or mice, or any animal, for that matter."

"I understand, Stepmother. They are beasts, after all."

Guinevere faced the little princess, eyebrows raised. "Exactly my thoughts, little one."

Guinevere walked over to the ornate chest taking long, prideful strides, examining the intricate carvings on the sides. "Since you have so greedily commanded my absolute companionship, why don't you come over and open the chest, little princess?" Princess Guinevere placed her hands on her hips, irritated to be without servants.

"Of course, Stepmother." Zezolla kneeled beside the heavy chest unlocking the latch. She slowly opened the lid, exposing an array of gorgeous gowns made from the finest silk.

"Well, look how your father has spoiled you." Princess Guinevere leaned into the chest, rubbing the fabric through her fingers. Zezolla moved back in order to give her stepmother room to examine the dresses.

"Stepmother, which gown is your favorite? I will wear that one first."

Guinevere pulled out a few gowns as she lay them out on the floor. "Well, these are all lovely, but I'm not sure if they are worthy for a little princess. After all, we must maintain appropriate appearances." She continued shifting the dresses around, leaning further inside the chest. Zezolla placed her hands on the heavy lid, her heart racing. Lucifer meowed at the little princess, encouraging her to proceed. Zezolla glanced at the cat, her breath quickening. "I can't, Lucifer," she whispered.

"What was that? Did you say something to that cat?" Guinevere looked up at Zezolla as she quickly removed her hands from the lid.

"No, Stepmother. I was saying that I have the lid."

Guinevere returned to her treasure hunt, muttering spiteful words as she continued. "Children... Why would anyone want such bothersome creatures?" Lucifer hissed at Zezolla, indicating that time was running out. Once again, Zezolla grabbed the lid, bracing herself for what she was required to do. "I found it. The gown you should wear." Guinevere began to emerge from the chest. Zezolla slowly released her fingers from the lid, never taking her eyes off of her stepmother's neck. "I can't do it, Lucifer. This is wrong."

"What is the matter with you child? Are you as brain dead as you are wicked?" She laughed into the chest. "Dear me, a retarded hexe! Who ever heard of such a pathetic thing?" Lucifer jumped off the bed, landing on Zezolla's hands, his claws dug deep into the princess's fingers. She screeched out in pain, slamming the lid as Lucifer tore at her flesh. Blood splattered onto Zezolla's face. She screamed in horror as her stepmother's dead body sat motionless outside the chest, her severed head trapped inside.

"Raven, raven! Come to me!" Zezolla cried. Her faithful pet flew through the window, staring at the display before him.

"It is done, Princess. There is nothing you can do now."

Zezolla hugged her raven as she sobbed into his wings. "I wasn't going to do it. I wasn't going to go through with it, but Lucifer-he jumped on my hands." She showed the raven her bloody fingers, the revolting gash marks extending from her fingertips to her knuckles. The raven watched as Lucifer retracted his claws, sauntering through the passage back to his mistress.

"Princess, this is not your fault. You have the marks of the cat to prove your innocence to your father. Tell him you were holding the lid when the cat saw a mouse and jumped on your hands. You let go out of pain, resulting in the decapitation of your stepmother. They cannot fault you, Princess. It will be declared an accident, and all will be in the past." Zezolla held on to her bird, cradling him as she cried.

The governess entered the room, smirking silently at the scene of horror. "Oh, my sweet little princess. You murdered your stepmother!" she exclaimed, pretending to be shocked.

Zezolla lunged into her stepmother's dress, clinging to her body. "No, Governess, I did not. It was an accident and I didn't mean to do it." Her words were unrecognizable through her cries. She was hysterical and shaking as she begged for her governess to help her.

"Don't worry, little princess. Your secret is safe with me. I will never tell your father or the king that you killed your stepmother."

"B-but I," stammered Zezolla, "but you told me-"

"Shh... Be calm now. No point in lying to the one person who loves you in this cruel world. I am the only one you can trust, the only person who cares for you. I will keep you safe." Zezolla, being only a child, believed her governess's words. "Thank you, Governess, thank you! Please don't let them kill me. Please protect me." The governess cooed to the little princess, embracing her trembling form as she spoke. "I will keep you safe, my little love, but I will need your help. I cannot protect you forever, not as your governess. In order for me to keep you eternally safe, I will need to be your new stepmother."

Zezolla looked up at her savior. "But how? You are just a governess. Father would never marry a governess."

She smiled at the pathetic child before her. "He will, Princess, once he discovers you know the truth about your mother's death."

Death Has Come

True to her word, the governess kept Zezolla safe from the laws of the land. She testified to Prince Baldric and the king, saying she witnessed the horrific accident which took place in Zezolla's chamber herself. Prince Baldric's heart ached for his daughter, blaming himself for causing her such a traumatic ordeal. The king also sympathized with the tiny princess and concluded that it was indeed a tragic event. Prince Baldric and his daughter were allowed to stay in their castle and remain in the land. Consumed by gratitude, Prince Baldric honored his deceased wife with a grand funeral open to all the kingdom. The king was pleased with Prince Baldric's display of respect and informed Baldric he may marry again if he so wished under the condition that he may not take another princess for a bride. Prince Baldric respectfully agreed to the terms and organized a journey to Hungary to find an adequate duchess for his bride. On the eve of his departure, he paid his daughter a visit in the hopes of lifting her spirits that she soon would have a mother again.

Zezolla was sprawled out on her floor, wrapped up in a bear skin rug. She clung to her raven as if he were a stuffed animal. The light of the fire cast a warm glow upon the tiny princess.

"My sweet little love… All the horror you have seen in your young life. I am sorry for the recent events, but I will make it right by you. I am leaving at morning's first light to go to Hungary. There I will marry a duchess who will be your new stepmother."

Zezolla did not greet her father. Instead, she rose from her spot on the floor and carried her raven to the window, releasing him into the evening sky. She watched her raven, admiring him as he flew into the night, black amongst silver and blue. "I do not wish for a duchess to be my new stepmother, Father."

Taken aback by his daughter's response, he moved closer to the princess. "Darling, I understand you only want your mother, but I require a wife and you a woman to call mother."

"No, Father, you do not understand. I will have a new mother, but I will select her. Not you."

"How dare you speak to me that way! I am your father. I am The Lord of this castle, and you are a mere child! You do not give me orders."

Zezolla never took her eyes off of her majestic raven, longing for wings of her own to fly away. "You will marry my governess and make her my new stepmother, Father."

Prince Baldric cackled in disgust, spinning his daughter around.

"You listen to me, you little Hexe. I will never marry a common governess, let alone take orders from a brat! I have given you excuse after excuse and made practical arguments on your behalf, but it all stops now!"

Zezolla called her raven to her side. He entered the room, gracefully landing on her shoulder. "You will marry my governess and make her my new stepmother, or I will tell the truth about my mother's death."

Prince Baldric trembled, putting distance between him and his daughter. "You truly are a witch. How do you know about that?"

"With eyes and ears that you do not know I have, Father. How else?"

Her riddle sent chills down his spine. "Your mother? Do you commune with the dead?" Baldric felt a quiver in his leg, giving him the feeling that he might fall.

"My eyes and ears soar through the cloudiness of the sky. They see all, hear all, and know all, Father. You will marry my governess and you will marry her by tomorrow's first light." Zezolla walked towards her father, closing the gap between them. "If you do not, I will tell how you took my mother away from me. Considering how you recently lost a second wife the king will link you to his sister's death as well as my mother's. You will hang for two murders. You stole my birth mother from me, Father. You owe me a new mother and I choose my governess."

Prince Baldric married the Lady Tremaine that same night in a private ceremony within the castle. The only witness to the marriage was Zezolla. Her father never again interfered with his daughter's macabre ways. She remained in black with her loyal companion perched on her shoulders, barefoot, and wandering in solitude. In the evenings, Baldric stopped looking out the castle windows.

He pretended that his daughter wasn't outside roaming the grounds. He silenced the whispers amongst Zezolla's staff concerning her speaking to animals and making miniature graves in the castle garden. Baldric stayed in his quarters, seeing his new wife only during special occasions. He was not aware Lady Tremaine sent for her five daughters. He only noticed his new stepchildren one evening at dinner. Five girls sat around their mother, each dressed in expensive gowns. Prince Baldric did not care who the Lady Tremaine opened their castle to. She was no family of his and he was now utterly alone in the world.

The Lady Tremaine established her own wing in the castle, setting up a royal living space for her daughters. The sisters were all one year apart, starting with the eldest, Claudette, followed by Marguerite, Jacqueline, and ending with the twins Anastasia and Drusilla. Claudette and Jacqueline were the prettiest of the five, although all were rather plain. They were ordinary girls in need of schooling and lessons in the arts, yet they were confident and conceited. The girls felt entitled and believed life owed them rewards of wealth and nobility. They kept to themselves, boasting over their mother's cleverness for marrying a prince and living in a royal castle. Lady Tremaine was satisfied with her new-found success, but she was still not content. One more loose end to tie up before her ever after would be complete.

"Mother, why must that awful brat walk around in black? She's so uncivilized." Jacqueline stared at her stepsister as she walked to her stepmother's chamber.

"She is an inexcusable beast, isn't she?" Lady Tremaine stroked her cat as Zezolla entered the chamber. "Just follow my lead, my beauties... Not much longer now."

Claudette giggled as her stepsister bowed.

"Hello Stepmother... Stepsisters."

"Zezolla." Lady Tremaine bowed to her stepdaughter without a trace of love or kindness in her voice. "What brings you to our quarter of the castle? Shouldn't you be in your own wing, dear?"

Zezolla looked over at her stepsisters as they hovered together, giggling at her.

"I missed you, Stepmother. I wanted to visit." The girls burst into laughter, mocking Zezolla.

"I miss you, Stepmother. I wish I had a real mommy who loved me." Sang Claudette.

Anastasia turned to her twin, Drusilla. "Why can't I have a mommy of my own?"

"Because, Hexe, your mommy is dead. Your daddy killed her and now you are all alone," mocked Drusilla. The twins held hands, spinning around as they laughed.

"Girls, girls. Manners, my pets." Lady Tremaine smirked with amusement. "Run along now, little Princess. You do not belong with us."

Zezolla looked at her stepmother, longing for things to be the way they used to be. "You do not want me here, Stepmother?"

"GOD! How dense can you get?" Roared Claudette. "Of course we don't want you here!"

Marguerite swatted at Zezolla like she was an annoying fly. "Go away now. You are growing bothersome and mother is tired."

Lady Tremaine laughed at her daughter's cruelness, shrugging her shoulders at Zezolla. "You heard her, my darling daughters. Run along now, Princess, you cannot come back here."

It was no surprise to Zezolla when her father became gravely ill three months later with the fever. Everyone knew he only had days before he would die and Zezolla foresaw his demise. Just like her, he was a nuisance to The Lady Tremaine. Prince Baldric no longer held any importance for her stepmother. Zezolla had blindly aided her stepmother's ultimate plan, becoming the lady of the castle and sealing her daughters' security in wealth. Zezolla concluded it would be only a matter of time before her own murder would take place. Zezolla never visited her father as he lay dying in his bed. Still heartbroken over her mother, Zezolla believed her father got what he deserved. She sent her raven to check in on him, keeping a watchful eye on his physical state.

"Your stepmother is tending to him, little princess. She is feeding him a tonic. Poison, no doubt."

Zezolla listened, stroking her raven's ebony wings, never showing any hints of emotion. "Hmm, yes, I believe you are correct, my raven. It will be a painful death indeed."

The raven hopped onto his princess's arm. "Not as painful as drowning by the hands of your own husband, my little princess."

"No. That is very true, raven. He had this coming."

A private funeral was held. Only the Lady Tremaine, her daughters, and Zezolla attended. Zezolla sat by her father's grave as she watched a worm find its way into the earth. Silence filled the air. All was calm and quiet. Lady Tremaine stood on top of the hill. She would never again return to her dead husband's grave.

Zezolla stayed by the freshly dug grave wishing her father could have been a better man. One she could have grieved for. "The world does not mourn my father. His spirit has been taken and all is as it should be, my love."

"Not all is quiet. Look, little princess, the king's royal carriage is approaching."

"Why is the king here? Do you suppose he might evict us from the castle now that Father is dead?"

"I don't know, little princess. Let's hope not."

The king made his way to Lady Tremaine and her daughters. Each girl curtsying in their clumsy way, giggling as the young king strode up to their mother. "Hush now. You will make fools of us. Try to act like ladies for once." Lady Tremaine gracefully bowed. "Your Majesty. How kind of you to honor my husband's memory by coming to our humble funeral."

"Lady Tremaine, a word if I may." Said the king. He looked over at the giggling girls. "In private."

"Of course, Your Majesty. Away with you, daughters." The girls ran up the hill, hiding behind a tree.

"Lady Tremaine, I am in dismay over the recent death of Prince Baldric. This castle must be cursed to have seen so many deaths in such a short time."

"It is a lovely castle, Your Grace. Such a tragedy that death has come here in these dark days."

"Yes, Indeed." The king glanced at Prince Baldric's grave.

"I have come to talk about the princess."

"Zezolla, Your Majesty?"

"Her name is Princess Zezolla, Lady Tremaine. Do not forget that girl is royalty and you, my dear lady, are not." The king pointed to the girls hiding behind the tree. "And neither are they."

"Yes, Your Majesty, of course. The Princess Zezolla, my beloved stepdaughter."

The king leaned into Lady Tremaine, towering above her. "You may stay in this castle as long as Princess Zezolla remains here. The day she leaves to marry, you and your daughters will be evicted from this house of royalty. I will leave it up to Princess Zezolla where to place you and your girls when the time comes. Your fate lies in your beloved stepdaughter's hand. Treat her well, Lady Tremaine, and pray your kindness towards her through the years will reward you with a wealthy life."

Lady Tremaine held her tongue, repressing the animosity stirring inside her. She hated her stepdaughter. She wanted her in a grave next to her father. She never had intentions of raising and keeping Zezolla as her own and now her plans were spoiled. This unexpected twist of events meant Zezolla would have to remain alive and occupy the castle or Lady Tremaine and her daughters would be cast into the streets, penniless, and without a home.

The king walked over to the little princess. Zezolla sat mute and tired, deep in thought. She did not wish to speak to the king, or to anyone, for that matter. Solitude suited her.

"My little princess."

Zezolla began to rise but the king stopped her. "It's alright, princess, remain as you are."

"Thank you, my king."

"I am sorry you have lost your father, little one. You've had some terrible losses in your young life."

"I am sorry for your loss as well, my king, for you to have lost someone you loved."

The king was impressed by the little princess's maturity. He reached down, touching Zezolla's hair. "You have ginger hair. I never noticed the color under your black ribbon you keep it in."

Zezolla continued to stare at her father's grave. "I do not like the color," she answered honestly.

"That's odd to say. Ginger is a beautiful color."

"I wish it black as raven's wings."

The king stood amazed by the princess. "I don't believe I've ever seen a beautiful woman with raven black hair. All the women in my kingdom have fair hair with light eyes."

"Then you've never seen true beauty, Your Majesty."

The king laughed at the little princess, kneeling down. "I'll tell you what, little Princess. If I ever meet a beautiful woman in my kingdom with raven black hair, I will make her my bride."

The princess looked over at the kind king kneeling beside her. "One day you shall meet a beauty with raven black hair. Please remember me when you, do Your Majesty."

Her Name Is Cinderella

Years passed. Lady Tremaine ruled the castle as if it were her own kingdom. She told no one of the king's orders. As long as Zezolla remained in the castle, so would the Lady Tremaine. She used her time as the head mistress of the castle to prepare her daughters to be eligible to marry a man of royalty. To ensure that Zezolla would not spoil her plans, she was banished to the cellar of the castle to live underground amongst the mice and rats who occupied it. Zezolla never complained. She welcomed the freedom from her stepmother and stepsisters. She preferred to live in the darkness with the rodents, her devoted raven was also always by her side. Time passed and word spread of the king's marriage to an older princess in the region. Her father was a king of great wealth. Joining their kingdoms brought immense prosperity to the land. Lady Tremaine never received another visit from the king, and she began to no longer fear the threats he had made by her husband's grave. She lived in security, never fretting the end of her time as the head lady of Hinterhohen Castle. She even began to forget about the princess who lived in the cellar.

Zezolla lost everything she owned to her stepsisters. She was only allowed to keep what her small hands could hold. Her greedy step-sisters took all her belongings;

gorgeous gowns, beautiful jewelry, expensive cosmetics, and her collection of games. However, Zezolla had no real attachment to those material objects. All she had wanted was her sacred hazel branch and a shard of glass from her mother's last gift; the now broken glass doll.

"Princess. I have a gift for you." Her raven flew in through the cellar door carrying a package in his beak.

"What wonderful present do you have for me, my love?"

The raven dropped the package at Zezolla's feet. She carefully opened the burlap. "It's perfect, my raven! The fabric is a gorgeous black just like your wings." She kissed the raven on his beak. "I think I now have enough to make another dress." She walked to the corner of the room and placed the fabric with the other pieces her raven had brought her. "I'm sorry that you have to steal it, my love. I made you a promise all those years ago and I have failed to keep it."

"No, my princess, you have kept it. You share your diminutive meals with me. You sneak me treats instead of keeping the delicious fruit for yourself. I am a thief by nature, my sweet Princess. I will always be a thief in one way or another."

"And I will always have darkness in me, my love. That's why we are perfect for each other." The princess sat down on the cold stone floor and sewed the scrap pieces of fabric together to make a cloak. "It is getting colder out, my love. I think a cloak will suit my needs more than a new dress."

The raven rested his head on the princess's shoulder as she worked, singing a bittersweet melody of loss and love. "You still miss her, my princess."

"Every moment of every day, my love."

"Perhaps now is the opportune time to plant your mother's branch" suggested the raven.

Zezolla swung her cloak in the air. "There. It is complete." She announced proudly.

"Try it on, my princess."

She stood, swinging the cloak around her slender body.

"It is beautiful. Just like you, my princess."

"Will you walk with me amongst the stars, my love?"

"I will always accompany you into the dark, my Princess."

Zezolla grabbed her mother's twig, her black raven perched on her shoulders. "Let us do some magic this night, my raven. You and I."

The night air frosted the ground as Zezolla walked. 'Midnight crystals' is what she called the cold earth beneath her bare feet. The earth showed its alliance to Zezolla by never stinging her exposed skin from the cold as she ventured further into the garden. She thanked nature, whispering gentle words of praise to the beloved world around her. Five grand boulders guarded the entrance to the forest, protecting the life inside from any evil that sought to destroy it.

"Are we going into the forest, my princess?" Asked the raven.

"Yes, my love. We are."

71

"How are we to pass through the boulders? They are too big for you to climb and have no passage from the side."

Zezolla couldn't go up or around the massive barrier. She walked to each side of the boulders, weighing out her options. "Since I do not have wings to fly over, I will have to make a way through for myself." She picked up a sharp rock and cut of a lock of her hair. She placed the hair into the center of the boulder, making a wide circle in the dirt. "What cannot fly above or walk around, what must be journeyed in-between, make me a passage into your keep!" Zezolla looked down, seeing the earth shift. A crack formed in the center as the boulders exposed a narrow path. She held up her hands again and offered her gratitude to nature for hearing and granting her request. "My thanks to you, Queen of Life. I will live to serve you and only you. You have my devotion until my last dying breath." The raven marveled at Zezolla's magical abilities. "You have developed into a grand witch, my lovely princess. Your mother will be proud."

Sleep had not come to all in the castle that night. There were others awake noticing Zezolla's journey into the dark. "Jack," barked Eleanor, "Jack! Wake up, you silly man!"

"What is it now, Eleanor?" Moaned Jack.

"The princess is at it again. She is walking around barefoot, heading to the forest." She said as she peaked out the window.

The servant turned to her husband. "Who walks around barefoot in the cold?"

"Hexe does." Answered Jack. He rolled onto his stomach.

"What do you want me to do about it? That girl is not right."

"Follow her," said his wife.

"Woman, you've gone mad! I'm not leaving my bed to follow a witch into the forest."

"Take Edward with you" instructed Eleanor.

Jack moaned, pulling the covers over his head. "Get up now, you useless man, and get Edward!" She pushed her husband out of bed. "Now! Before she goes further out onto the grounds."

"Curse you, woman!" Cried Jack. "If I had been born of nobility, I never would have married a wretch like you." Reluctantly, Jack did as he was told and set off to collect Edward from the adjoining servants' room, knowing that his wife would never allow him a moment's sleep if he disobeyed. As with Jack, Edward's wife already had him up and dressed. Edward frowned at Jack, grabbing his lantern. "Come on," mumbled Edward. "The sooner we leave the sooner we can be back in our beds." Edward was a young man, only married a few years. He knew, like everyone else, that the forest had been secured off with no possible way inside.

"Our wives are just allowing their imagination to run away from them" said Edward. "There is no way to gain entrance into the forest. That girl probably just went to the edge and turned around. We won't be gone more than a few minutes before we run into her venturing back." The air was frigid. A gust of wind emerged from the forest, chilling the servants as they walked.

"Hexe has always roamed the night in secret. We all know she's a witch. What do our wives want from us?" Edward was annoyed by their wives' obsession over Zezolla's behavior. He was tempted to turn around and tell his wife that Zezolla had returned back to the castle, but he knew better than to lie to her.

"Eleanor is afraid of the girl. She says Zezolla killed her stepmother." Jack raised the lantern to Edward's face, casting a ghostly shadow upon his skin. "She says she saw Princess Guinevere's blood on Hexe's face and hands. Zezolla slammed the lid on that poor princess, cutting off her own stepmother's head. You and Libby are new, and you weren't here when the other servants fled in terror after the death of Princess Guinevere."

"If she's so terrifying, why are you still here?" Edward was still unconvinced Zezolla was dangerous.

"I'm not afraid of Hexe. I know she won't hurt us as long as we stay out of her way. But coming out here in the night after her is a grave mistake. You mark my words Edward, this could be the nail in our coffin."

Edward dismissed Jack's warning. "The only woman I am worried about burying me six feet under is my wife. Let's just find out what Zezolla is up to so that we can go back to bed." He groaned. "Those damn girls will have us up at the crack of dawn doing their bidding and I need sleep." He looked down at the footprints leading into the forest. "Lady Tremaine's daughters are the real witches we should be worrying about."

Zezolla entered the forest, twig in one hand, shattered glass in the other. She moved effortlessly through the night as if she herself had wings to carry her. She came to a clearing, a streak of moonlight shining on the frozen ground. "This is the spot, my love." The raven flew into the sky circling Zezolla as she dug into the ground.

"Remember the order, my princess. Plant the twig and then the glass."

Zezolla nodded.

"I call upon the spirit of my mother. I command you to leave the grave in which my mother's body rests. Awaken now and bring forth the tree of life!" Zezolla held her hands up to the moon, invoking its powers. "I am the daughter of the witch Avelina. I invoke the powers of the night. Come to me, my mother's spirit. I welcome you!"

A silver mist traveled above. The raven flew down to his princess. "She is coming, Princess."

Zezolla watched as the mist descended down to the ground, landing on the bed of earth. The mist began to rise up from the earth, swirling like a twister, faster and faster. It spun, causing the wind to pick up and howl as the twister grew. Zezolla stayed grounded with her arms extended and her head held up to the moon. Lighting crashed down from the sky, hitting the earth. The trees were swaying around her, calling to her mother's spirit.

"My princess, look…look at the ground."

Zezolla watched as a tiny branch came forth from the dirt. Slowly it grew, taller and taller spreading its branches in every direction. Zezolla thought she saw the figure of a woman in the tree. Shards of glass fused together creating glass leaves, dangerous to anyone who touched it –

anyone but Zezolla. The princess stood up, amazed by the beautiful sight before her. "It is complete, my love. My mother is here, and her spirit resides within this tree." A remarkable Hazel tree stood before her, 15 feet tall with a small opening at the base big enough for Zezolla to fit through. She examined the leaves while running her long fingers over the glass. "It cannot cut me, my love." She held out her arm for the raven to perch upon. "But it will be dangerous for anyone else who tries to touch it."

The two men made it to the barrier, gasping in horror. "What entrance is this!?" Exclaimed Jack. "This was never here. There has never been an entrance to the forest." Jack backed away, terrified that Zezolla had awakened a spirit inside the forest.

"It's just a narrow passage. It must have been caused by the cold ice." Concluded Edward logically.

Jack shook his head. "No, Hexe did this. She has opened the forest. Who knows what evil lurks inside? These grounds are now cursed. I will not venture inside." Jack turned to leave but Edward stopped him. "This might be valuable to me, Jack. If Hexe possesses some magical entity inside the forest, then I want it."

Edward grabbed Jack by the collar and moved him through the opening. Jack clung to his knife, jumping at the sounds around them. "There is a light coming from beyond the trees. Could be lightening. Let's go see what Hexe is up to." Jack tried to turn back once again, but Edward had a strong hold on him. "Courage, man! You're no better than a scared boy." Snarled Edward.

Zezolla, unaware of the servants approaching, entered the hazel tree. Jack ducked down behind a bush as he saw Zezolla disappear.

"We must leave now! I told you this would be our demise! She is a witch! Did you not just see how she entered that glass tree?!"

Edward was too fascinated to leave. He had never witnessed true magic before. "I want to take a closer look."

"What? Are you mad! If you go near that tree that will be the end of you!"

Edward did not listen to Jack and walked over to the magical tree which was shimmering in the moonlight. "I just want to see it. Stay where you are if you are afraid," Edward snorted.

"To hell with curiosity. I don't want to end up without my head like Princess Guinevere. Go on then, you fool! Go see your magical tree."

The tree seemed to call to Edward, beckoning him forward. "It's so beautiful. Look at the sparkling leaves." He reached out to touch one. The branch moved, slicing his finger off his hand. Edward screamed in pain, clenching his mutilated hand to his chest. He tried to run away, but the tree caught him in her branches.

Jack stayed hidden, watching in horror as Edward cried out for help. "Jack, help me!"

"Stupid fool. I told him not to get closer." Muttered Jack horrified by what he was witnessing.

The tree tightened its grip around Edward, cutting him as it squeezed. "Please! I am sorry! Please let me go!" The tree would not accept Edwards pleas and brought down another branch lined with razor sharp leaves. "No! No! Please, I will do anything! I will protect the princess from her stepmother. I swear to protect her as long as I live! Please, spare me!" The branch came down, slicing Edwards throat with a row of deadly leaves.

"She needs no protection. I am with her now." Said the tree as Edwards body fell..

Jak ran after hearing the words spoken by the tree. He fled, running straight back to the castle, fleeing the terrible sight under the magic tree. He rushed to his wife, throwing their belongings in a sack.

"Jack... Jack!! What is it? What happened?" asked Eleanor as she jumped out of bed.

"Pack, woman. We are leaving this place tonight!"

"What about Edward?"

"Edward was a fool and he now lies dead in the forest. We must go, now, before Hexe comes back. Go fetch his wife, if you wish, but if you are not outside in five minutes time, I will leave you here, woman! This is all your fault!"

Zezolla made her way down the tree's winding staircase. "It mirrors the tree my mother had in our former castle, my love."

"Yes, Princess, Avelina has given you your own place of magic. Here you will be protected from unwelcomed eyes while you grow in your magical abilities."

Zezolla smiled, cooing at her raven. "It is perfect, isn't it, my love? This shall bring new life to our world."

"Yes, my Princess. You will do great good for the earth and the creatures who reside on her.."

"I hope so, my love. I only want to bring blessings to those who need them." She looked down at the wooden table, running her delicate hand across it. "I have seen enough pain and wickedness to last into my next life."

Zezolla awoke to bells ringing in her cellar. Her stepmother was up and this was her way of requesting Zezolla's immediate presence. Zezolla ran up the stairs where her stepmother and stepsisters waited at the landing.

"What have you done?" Roared Lady Tremaine.

Zezolla looked at her stepmother. "I did nothing, stepmother."

"Don't you lie to me, Hexe, you scared off my servants!"

Zezolla then noticed her stepmother and stepsisters were still in their sleeping gowns. "The servants have gone, stepmother?" She asked, bewildered.

"Imbecile! Isn't that what I just said? I know you did something. You scared off the first lot of servants with your bizarre ways and now this group has fled in the middle of the night, leaving us without servants once again!"

"I can go into town, Stepmother, and find you other servants."

"That will not suffice, Hexe. No one will come and work for me, not for the little pay I offer. These were the last remaining fools who would stay." She paced back and forth, rage clouding her eyes. Lady Tremaine stopped and looked down at her stepdaughter. "You. You will be our servant." She pointed a long, bony finger at Zezolla.

"Me? But I've never taken care of anyone in my life! I do not know how to do all the chores that you require." Zezolla protested.

"Then you shall learn, my pet. Girls… Show our new servant how to dress a lady for morning tea." The daughters laughed, eager to have a princess do their bidding.

"Yes, Mother" replied Jacqueline. "We will make sure to show our new servant how to dress a real lady." Marguerite giggled as she twirled around, joining in the fun. "Come, servant. My dress requires pressing before you clothe me."

"Ours too!" Chimed in the twins.

"And I require a morning bath, servant girl." Added Claudette. "If my bath water is the least bit cold, I will drown you in the tub as punishment."

"You cannot do this, Stepmother. I am a princess. I am not a servant!" Cried Zezolla.

Lady Tremaine walked down the stairs, grabbing Zezolla by the neck. "I can and I will. You are no princess in this castle. It's been years since the king has even remembered your existence. If you do not want to end up on the streets as a beggar, then you will do as I command! I am the queen in this castle." She turned Zezolla's face to her stepsisters "and they are your princesses. Don't be mistaken about that, dear stepdaughter."

Zezolla learned quickly how to serve her stepsisters. Every morning before dawn Zezolla awoke to prepare for the tedious and demanding day ahead. She pressed her stepsisters dresses, prepared their baths, combed their hair, did the washing, the cooking, the mending, the sewing, and constantly swept the firesides in each of her stepsisters' bedrooms. Zezolla never let her stepsisters see the worst of her. Through all the demands and orders, Zezolla remained forever stoic, and all the while her stepsisters' cruelty intensified. With each day that passed, the stepsisters' wickedness toward Zezolla grew. Every morning was a new game for the girls. Who could be the cruelest to their servant? What new and splendid ways could they find to humiliate her?

Zezolla was bent over, cleaning the fireplace, her ginger hair black from the soot. Drusilla walked into her room after music lessons. She called for her twin. "Anastasia, come here, come look at our cinder slave."

Anastasia fell over laughing. "Her hair is trashed! It's covered in ash and soot!"

The other sisters ran over to join in on the fun. "Imagine having your hair covered in cinder! It's ghastly!" Sang Marguerite.

"Ew. Never to be kissed by a fella, if you've touched Cinderella." Chanted Anastasia.

Drusilla was rolling on the ground, unable to stop her laughter. "Cinderella!" She cried, amused by the nickname.

"Come here, Cinderella," ordered Claudette, her hands resting on her hips, her cold eyes staring at her.

Zezolla walked over, obeying her cruel stepsister. "Turn around, Cinderella."

Zezolla did as she was told, turning around for her stepsister. "Her hair is disgusting. How is she ever going to get all of that soot out?" Anastasia went to touch the black knots tangled in her hair.

"God no! Don't touch it, sister!" Marguerite stopped Anastasia, revealing a pair of shears.

"The only way to get out soot from Cinderella's hair is to cut it off." Marguerite said darkly.

Zezolla tried to turn around to stop Marguerite from cutting her hair, but the other girls grabbed Zezolla and held her down on the floor, her face in a pile of soot. "Keep her still!" Screamed Marguerite. She sat on top of Zezolla, snipping off locks of her hair.

Zezolla stopped fighting as she knew there was no point. If they wanted her hair, they would have it eventually. She stared off into the world outside, watching her raven fly freely amongst the clouds. "At least one of us is free," she thought.

That evening, Zezolla returned to her cellar, looking for her raven. When she did not see him, she donned her cloak and walked into the night hoping that he would be waiting for her by the forest. "Come to me, my love." Zezolla held out her arm, waiting for her raven to join her.

"My princess. Your eyes are sorrowful tonight. What has happened?" Zezolla spoke not a word but continued into the forest, seeking comfort from her mother. The tree immediately opened its branches upon her arrival, revealing the secret passage. "Princess, will you not talk to me?" Asked her raven. Zezolla walked down the winding staircase, placing her bird on to a branch. She lit the candles, still keeping her silence. "My princess, I am speaking to you. Why will you not acknowledge me?"

Zezolla finally faced her raven, removing the hood from her head. "My name is not Princess Zezolla anymore, my love, for now I am Cinderella."

Black as Raven's Wings

Cinderella's ginger hair was chopped close to her skull. Patches of honey were all that remained of her lovely locks. Blood still dripped from the fresh wounds and her raven wanted to heal the sores to erase the pain the vile sisters had afflicted on Zezolla. His heart broke for his princess. She did not deserve to be treated so viciously.

"My princess, I am so sorry they did this to you. Those malevolent girls do not deserve to walk freely in this world." She lowered her head so he could caress her scalp with his wing. "It does not matter what they call you or what they take from you. You, are my princess, my Zezolla, and you always will be." The raven plucked a black feather from his body. "A gift for you, my princess. Use it and you will find completion once again."

Zezolla took the black feather and placed it into her cauldron. She added the eye of a toad, scales from a fish, and a pinch of dirt from her mother's new grave. She turned around, fingering the jars on the shelves. "I'm missing something..." She held a candle up to the jars carefully reading the labels.

"What is it you seek princess?"

"The blood of a man." Her eyes locked on to a vial. "A man whom this tree has claimed for its own." She emptied the entire thing into the cauldron. Flames erupted and a scream arose from the potion.

"Is that scream from the servant, my princess?"

"I believe so, my love. He must not have been good man. Mother always has reasons for her actions and must had them for ending his life. I did not understand why she would murder him at first, but she allowed me to see inside his heart. He was dark, my love, so very dark. He took pleasure in hurting young girls. He stalked his victims, considering each one nothing more than a trophy. He wanted to use my magic for his own twisted pleasures, and with my power, he would have been unstoppable. That man did not deserve his life for he had stolen the lives of many young girls in this world. That scream was his corrupted soul leaving this earth."

Zezolla rose, closing her eyes as she connected with the energy surrounding her. "I call on the spirit of my mother. Turn my stepsisters' malicious joke for my benefit. Bless me with the hair of a raven, black and strong, so that no one may ever take it from me again!" Zezolla rubbed the potion on to her scalp, chanting as she worked. Zezolla's remaining ginger hair turned black as night. The more she chanted, the longer it grew. Her hair flowed from her head past her slender shoulders to her breasts, stopping finally at the small of her back.
"I am Zezolla no more, my love. I, am now Cinderella."

"But, Princess, why would you keep a name they cursed you with?"

"It was not a curse, my love, but a blessing. I am black as soot…I am dark as night…my ginger hair is no more. I finally have my raven's wings." She picked up her raven. "I owe all this to my stepsisters. By greeting them tomorrow with my raven hair and embracing my accepted name, I will send fear into their hearts and they will learn that I am a girl no more." She kissed her raven's beak, placing him on her shoulder. "Come, my love, let us rest before the sun arises." The raven nestled into her thick mane and realized his little princess was indeed no longer a girl.

At breakfast, the stepsisters sat around the table mocking Cinderella. "Cinderella! After breakfast, comb my long, beautiful locks." Claudette was blessed with long flowing hair, the color of sunshine.

Cinderella bowed to her stepsister, her hair pinned back with a thick black ribbon. "As you command, stepsister."

The other girls laughed, whispering dramatically to each other. "We should bring her back to Claudette's room and make her tend to the fireplace." Snickered Jacqueline. "Once she's on her hands and knees, we will rip off her ribbon and show mother how hideous our Cinderella really is."

Jacqueline was proud of her simple yet humiliating plan.

"Excellent idea, sister" said Marguerite. "Won't Mother be pleased to see how we've groomed our pet?" Cinderella showed no emotion as she served her stepsister, listening to their mockery. "She must be so

86

hideous now that she can't even walk within the castle walls without her black ribbon." Smirked Drusilla.

She turned to her twin. "It's not like a handsome prince will barge into the castle and demand to marry his true love, Princess Cinderella."

Anastasia chimed in, "oh, but a princess must always be prepared for her Prince Charming. With her head covered, he won't notice that his fair love has has *such* a lovely mane."

As Cinderella poured a cup of tea for her stepsister, Anastasia dug her heel into Cinderella's apron, tearing it off as she walked away. "Oh, poor Cinderella, did you lose your royal rags?"

Marguerite stood up. "Oh sissy, you can be so clumsy. Here, Cinderella, let me help you." She took hold of Cinderella's dress and cut the shoulder straps off with a knife, pieces of black fabric falling to the ground. "Oops. I am so sorry, stepsister, did I just ruin your only dress?" Laughter roared through the dining room.

Lady Tremaine walked in, eyeing the spectacle before her. "Girls!"
Her daughters immediately fell quiet returning to their chairs. "Let us not strip the poor child naked." She walked over to her stepdaughter eyeing her exposed shoulders. "If you cannot dress like a proper lady and keep your skin covered, you will force me to treat you like the dog that you are. Go and find some burlap to cover you skin or you will be sleeping with the pigs in the barn."

Cinderella bowed, her face ever stoic and calm. "Yes, stepmother" was her only reply. Lady Tremaine sat down

87

at the head of the table with a cup of tea. "A bit of morning fun my daughters?" She smiled, pleased with her girl's cruelness. "Let us make sure." She paused… "Cinderella, is it now?" The girls nodded, their faces brimming with pride. "Yes, let us make sure Cinderella is aware that she is no longer a princess in this castle. Those days of royalty are gone. She is nothing but our cinder girl."

Cinderella returned to the cellar, allowing her dress to fall to the floor. She had no shame in revealing her bare skin. She was comfortable with her nakedness; clothes were just a social necessity.

"My princess, let me help you with your dress." The raven took his claw and lifted the shards of fabric that hung behind Cinderella.

"It's not mendable, my love, not without more fabric. I will have to find something else to use as a dress."

"I shall return shortly, princess. Just wait here." The raven flew out of the cellar, leaving Cinderella to sit naked on the cold floor. She heard a shuffling sound coming from the wall. Cinderella crawled towards the noise, noticing a tiny hole. "Hello, is there someone inside?" A tiny mouse came out resting on its hind legs. "Well, aren't you a clever mouse? You have found yourself a safe part of the castle. Lucifer never ventures down here." Cinderella extended her hand toward the mouse, stroking its head. "You are welcome to stay as long as you like. I welcome the company." The mouse scurried back inside the hole, returning quickly with bits of black fabric. "For me, mouse?" Cinderella took the fabric, holding it up. "Is there anymore?" Again, the mouse ventured into the hole and returned three more times. "Why, this is perfect. Thank you, kind sir." She looked around the room. "I wish I had something to offer you in return, but I do not own much." The mouse bowed, indicating no gift of thanks was required. "I'll tell you what, my little pet. I believe I may have a few shreds of fabric left over. If I do, I will make you a soft bed stuffed with straw to sleep on. Would that suffice?" The mouse again bowed, and Cinderella knew he would be pleased with the present. She stroked the mouse one more time before he ran back into his hole.

Her raven returned with another ball of fabric. She spent the next hour mending her dress and apron. True to her word she used the spare bits of fabric to make the mouse a tiny bed. "I must leave you my love. Claudette has summoned me to comb her hair." The raven did not like being separated from his princess. He longed for the days when it was just them. "I shall return to you as soon as I can."

"My princess, I hate watching those evil girls mock you. It breaks my heart."

"Don't worry, my love." She stroked her raven, admiring his beautiful wings. "They cannot hurt me. In the end, fate will be their judge."

Claudette waited impatiently in her chamber. Devious thoughts roamed through her head. "What took you so long? You had me sitting here for almost an hour. My beautiful hair is in tangles!" Cinderella bowed as she entered her stepsister's room.

"Not like you have to fret over your hair needing grooming." Claudette smirked as she sat at her vanity. Her tiny nose turned upright. "Now brush my hair." Cinderella walked over to her stepsister, comb in hand. Claudette grabbed Cinderella's hand, digging her nails into her flesh. "Don't pull or I will strike you with the comb you hold."

"I understand, stepsister."

Claudette boasted about her beauty as Cinderella mechanically brushed, separating the strands of golden hair. "Mother says I will be attending a ball at the castle soon. She believes the king will notice me immediately and we shall fall in love. Everyone knows I am the loveliest out of all my sisters." Cinderella, not being privy to latest gossip, did not realize the king was looking to marry. Last she remembered he'd had a wife. "That worthless queen finally became pregnant with a child but lost the baby. Now she is barren and too old to give the king any more babies. He has annulled the marriage and sent her to live in Spain, leaving him free to marry once more. I will become queen." Boasted Claudette.

Cinderella mused over the current events, finding it sad and pathetic that a woman could be banished from her home, title stripped from her, and replaced by another who was more fertile. Claudette arose, pleased with her hair's silky condition. She turned to her stepsister, her face soft and tender. "My dear Cinderella. You have done so much for me. I would like to return the favor and brush your beautiful hair." She snatched the brush from Cinderella's hand and began to untie her black ribbon.

"No, my dear stepsister. I do not deserve your kindness. I am happy to serve you."

Claudette forcefully took her sister's head in her hands. "I insist, Cinderella." She unraveled the ribbon, a gloat of victory on her face. Cinderella did not protest but remained still as Claudette unwrapped the long ribbon. "What! What trickery is this?" Claudette jumped back, venom coursing through her veins. "Your hair! What have you done to your hair?" Cinderella cocked her head to the side, pretending she was oblivious to her stepsister's discovery. "You are a hexe! How else could you make it grow?" She took the back of the comb, striking Cinderella across the face. "Answer me, Hexe!" The other sisters stormed in, their mouths dropping at the spectacle before them. Cinderella stood glaring at her stepsisters, her thick, long hair trailing behind her.

"It's sorcery! It's a trick of magic!" Cried Jacqueline.

"No matter." Claudette reached for her shears. "What was done can be undone. Grab her, sisters." The girls forced Cinderella against the wall, her face pressed into the stones. Claudette took a chunk of black hair between the blades and cut, but to her surprise, the sheers broke. Not a strand of hair was severed. "Drusilla! Get me another pair of shears!" Drusilla returned with yet another pair of shears. The sister tried to cut the thick hair, but again, the shears broke. "What is this? Why won't it cut through your hair?"

Cinderella turned to face her stepsisters; her face victorious. "I gave you my ginger hair, stepsister. My raven hair is my own. You can never penetrate it for it is as strong as iron and black as night. No one shall take it from me again."

"I will tell mother about this!" Screamed Claudette.

Cinderella picked up her broom, walking to the door. "If you do tell stepmother about what I did, who do you think she will be more displeased with? Me? For casting magic of which you have no proof, or you for being outwitted by a servant?"

Claudette was furious the entire day. She knew Cinderella was right. If she did tell her mother about being outsmarted by Cinderella, then she too would be punished. Claudette sat in her room, devising a plan. "Come here, sweet Lucifer." The cat leapt onto the bed coming to a rest beside Claudette. "We know she's hiding something, don't we, Lucifer?" The cat purred encouragingly in response. "The only way to truly gain the upper hand with that witch is to catch her in the act. If I can find the place where she performs her dark magic, then I could set it aflame and really show that beast who is in control." Claudette rolled over on to her back. "How dare she grow her hair after I cut it? Who does that beast think she is?" Lucifer jumped on her stomach, kneading her with his paws. "What is it, Lucifer? Do you know where she goes at night to do the devil's work?"

Lucifer jumped off the bed, heading towards the hall. Claudette followed the black cat out into the courtyard. She saw Cinderella walking barefoot in the distance. "We must be quiet, Lucifer. I don't want the others to follow us. They might ruin the surprise." Claudette followed her stepsister through the cold night; darkness encompassing her as she tripped over tree limbs and stumbled over rocks. "How does that hexe walk barefoot through this forest without a lantern?"

Cinderella stopped along the way, looking up at the sky, watching her raven fly beneath the full moon. It was calming for Cinderella to be alone in the forest with nothing but her raven and nature to accompany her. Cinderella heard a small moan coming from behind a large rock. She walked around it and saw a gray wolf, his paw caught in a hunter's trap. "Are you injured, wolf?" The wolf lowered his head at the princess. "Can you move your paw at all?" The wolf shook his head no. Claudette hid behind a tree, watching as her stepsister moved closer to the animal.

"Is she mad? Watch her get eaten by the beast, serves her right walking up to a wild wolf!"

Cinderella kneeled beside the wolf, examining his paw. "It's caught tight, but I can free it." Cinderella cautiously reached for the trap, gripping the sides in both hands. "Stay perfectly still wolf, this will hurt."

The wolf laid his head on the ground, panting heavily. Cinderella pulled on the trap, releasing the wolf's paw. He howled in pain as she gently raised his paw removing, it from the metal claws. "There now, you're free, but you won't be able to move it. I can help mend it, but I will first need to find something to carry you on." Cinderella walked to the pumpkin patch growing nearby. "I wonder…" She trailed off, eyeing a pumpkin. "Come to me, my love." The raven flew down, landing on the pumpkin. "Will you find me a worm, my love?"

"As you wish, princess." The raven dug a hole in the ground, pulling up an earthworm with his beak. Cinderella took the worm and pricked her finger with a thorn and spat. She spread her blood and saliva on both the worm and the pumpkin. "My love, please peck a hole in the pumpkin." The raven did as Cinderella asked and pecked a small hole in the side of the pumpkin. Cinderella placed the worm by her foot. "First the pumpkin." She said. "I call on the spirit of my mother! Grow the pumpkin to hold a wolf and from my blood bring forth uncommon growth."

Cinderella watch in amusement as the pumpkin more than quadrupled in size. "Now for the worm." Cinderella placed the worm inside the hole. "Eat, worm." She commanded. Cinderella peeked inside the hole, eyeing the worm as it ate its way through the pumpkin and climbed out of the top. She stood back, giving the giant worm space. It crawled onto the ground next to her, squirming back into the earth from which it came. "Wolf, crawl inside the pumpkin so I may take you to my home." The wolf obeyed, curling his body into a ball.

"My princess, how do we transport the pumpkin to the castle?" Cinderella spotted some nuts dropped from a squirrel's nest. She picked up the nuts and again pricked her finger and rubbed the blood on the nuts. She extended her arms and cast a spell. "Grow these nuts twelve times their size. Make them big enough to be my wheels!" Her call was answered, and the nuts grew to be wheels. She attached them to the pumpkin and secured them in place with some ivy vines. She placed her hands on the ivy, ordering it to carry out her will. The ivy wrapped around the pumpkin, supporting the wheels and looping in the front as reins. Cinderella grabbed the ivy and pulled the pumpkin through the trees. It moved effortlessly for her. "Don't worry, young wolf, I shall bring you back to the castle and make you well again."

Claudette starred in amazement. "She is more powerful than I thought, Lucifer. I must stop her before her powers grow." Claudette waited until Cinderella was out of sight and then made her way to the sparkling tree. "This tree must be the source of her powers, Lucifer. If I burn it to the ground, then her powers will die with it." Lucifer stayed back, not wanting to get any closer. "Come on cat! It's just a tree." Lucifer did not listen and backed further away.

"Fine. Then I will go." She moved slowly, eyeing the sparkling leaves. "Crystals! That brat has grown a tree of jewels. Keeping her riches to herself, no less. Here my mother clothes, feeds, and houses that ungrateful beast and she is hiding riches from us." Lucifer screeched a meow warning Claudette not to touch the branches. Claudette stubbornly ignored Lucifer and proceeded to the hazel tree. "It's so beautiful! Look at all the crystals! We would be rich with this tree!" Claudette reached for one of the branches, mesmerized by the sparkling leaves. Her hand touched a leaf, pulling for it to come loose. "Ouch! It's so sharp!" She moved her hand away, staring at the blood pouring from her fingers. "It cut me. What kind of crystal is this sharp?" She reached again for the leaf, aiming for the smooth middle, avoiding the edges entirely, but again, her fingers were cut. "I don't understand. I did not touch the edge. How can it cut me?" Lucifer jumped on to a rock, hissing at Claudette. She turned to face him. "It must be a spell, bewitched to keep others from taking her treasure. Maybe I could break down some leaves by throwing rocks." Claudette collected a few rocks, aiming for the lowest branch. She threw the rocks at the leaves, but they just bounced off, quickly falling to the ground. "I should have known it wouldn't be that easy. She's enchanted it so only her greedy hands can get the crystals." Claudette sat next to Lucifer. "We shall wait for her to return and when she plucks the crystals from the tree, I will bash her head with a rock and collect the treasure for myself."

Meanwhile, Cinderella lay the wolf on a blanket, burning coal to keep him warm. "I can clean and dress your wound, but you will not be able to walk on it for a few days. I do not have much food, but I will do what I can to feed you." The wolf raised his head to the princess. "Is there something else you require, wolf?" The wolf placed his head between his legs and whined. "Please don't make any noise. If my stepmother discovers you, she will have you killed by the local hunters." Cinderella placed her hand on the wolf, stroking his gray fur. "I will be back shortly. Try to get some sleep. It will help you to heal." The wolf placed his paw on Cinderella's leg. She giggled. "I'm very happy I found you, wolf. I think we will be fast friends."

Cinderella returned to the forest, embracing the energy of the night. She felt alive whenever she used magic as if a piece of the universe flowed through her. "We will need to find some food for our new friend, my love, but first I must return to the hazel tree." Cinderella walked cautiously. A disturbing presence filled the forest. "We are not alone, my love. Someone else is here." The raven flew off into the night, scouting the area. Cinderella saw the figure of a woman standing beneath her tree. She watched silently as her stepsister circled the tree, a heavy rock in her hand. "I would not get any closer, stepsister, that tree has a mind of its own."

Claudette swirled around, facing Cinderella. "Don't tell me what to do, you greedy witch! You kept this tree hidden for yourself!" Claudette raised her rock at Cinderella. "Cut me down a branch so I may take the crystals back to mother or I will bash your head with this rock!" Claudette did not notice the hazel tree slowly move its branches around her body.

"Stepsister. I will warn you again. Move away from the tree. I am not able to control it. I cannot protect you from its wrath."

Claudette laughed at Cinderella's feeble attempts to frighten her. "You want the crystals for yourself. You will say anything to keep me from its riches." Cinderella eyed the tree, its long branches extending closer to Claudette. Razor sharp leaves glistened in the moonlight.

"Claudette! Move away now!"

Claudette raised the rock, aiming for her stepsister's head. "Come and make me, Hexe." Suddenly the tree closed its branches around Claudette. Its leaves cut into her flesh like barbwire. She screamed out in pain and the tree tightened its grip. Cinderella rushed to her stepsister, trying to remove the branches around her waist. "Help me! Cinderella, please do something!"

Cinderella's hand was sliced by the leaves. "I can't. She won't let me free you."

"What are you talking about? This is your tree! You can command it to stop! Please!" Blood was pouring from her waist as the tree dug deeper and deeper into her sides.

"I cannot control the tree. It is not me who commands it." She extended her hands, calling on the spirit of her mother. "Mother, please do not do this. Release my stepsister from your grasp! Spare her!" The tree shook in anger, digging deeper and deeper into Claudette. "Please! Stop mother, you are killing her!" Blood began to seep from Claudette's mouth.

"Cinderella! Please help me!" The hazel tree glowed with a bright silver light illuminating the night sky.

"Her name is Princess Zezolla. She is my daughter! She is of royal blood! You will die by my hands for the torment you have caused her!" Roared the tree.

Cinderella dropped to her knees as Claudette was sliced in half, her body still ensnared in the hazel tree. "Mother! What have you done?"

The hazel tree threw the body onto the ground. "Now you have food for your new pet, my daughter. Take half of her body back to the wolf but leave the remaining top. I owe a sacrifice to the night creatures."

Cinderella trembled, placing her hands over her eyes. "I can't. What will stepmother do when she finds out I fed her eldest daughter to my wolf?"

"She will never learn of this night. Send your raven to your evil stepmother. Have him whisper in her ear the cries of Claudette and let her think she came upon a hunter who mistook her for a beast and slaughtered her, her body being consumed by the bears who live in the forest."

Cinderella did as she was instructed, gathering the legs of her dead stepsister. "Mother, why? Why did you do this?"

"Your wolf needs food. He will serve you well, my daughter, and his protection will keep you alive in the future. Besides, this wicked girl did not deserve the gift of life. She abused you and her heart was black as coal. She met the very fate that she had in store for you. She was going to kill you, my daughter. If I were not here to save you, you would have met a similar death as she, your body feeding the wolves who roam the forest. Now go and think no more of what you saw." The tree released a silver mist covering Cinderella's head, all the sorrow and worry fleeing from her mind.

Lady Tremaine lay in her canopy bed, deep in slumber when the raven flew in. He perched by her side and began whispering in her ear. "Mother...mother. I have been slaughtered by a hunter."

Lady Tremaine shook in her sleep. "My daughter! What has happened to you?"

"I went into the night to gaze upon the royal castle. I was dreaming of becoming queen. A hunter spotted me and mistook me for a wild beast. He killed me, an arrow striking my heart. Before he knew his fatal mistake, a bear came upon him, slashing his throat and dragging him off into the forest."

"My daughter! Where is your body? Where will I find you?"

"You will never discover my body, mother. I, too, was dragged into the forest, meeting the same end as the hunter. Not even my bones will be discovered for they were consumed."

The raven flew from the dark room before the stepmother awoke, screaming in horror at the truth she had just dreamed. She ran through the halls, calling for Claudette all the while.

Cinderella placed a leg in front of the wolf, burning the clothes of her stepsister in the fire. "Here, my pet, nourishment for your body." The wolf greedily ate the leg, never looking up at Cinderella as he consumed the meaty flesh. "I have another for you, but it is buried in the forest. I could not bring it back to the castle. When you require more food, I will fetch it for you." The wolf bowed his head at his new mistress, his lips stained in blood. Cinderella lay beside the wolf, her raven asleep in her black hair. The wolf inched closer to his mistress, placing his head in her lap as she slept. He would remain loyal to Cinderella for all time.

One Down, Another to Go

The castle was filled with sorrow and torment the following weeks. Lady Tremaine took her grief out on Cinderella, lashing her with a walking cane when she did not complete her chores fast enough. Cinderella would return to her cellar at night with her back split open by the beatings. Her wolf offered comfort in these moments, lying down next to his mistress and licking her wounds as she trembled in pain. Her loyal raven would venture into the forest during the day, collecting herbs that could heal his beloved.

"My princess, I have brought you more herbs for your wounds" said the raven gently. Cinderella, barely able to move from pain and exhaustion, forced herself to mix the herbs in a mortar so her raven could spread the paste onto her wounds. "You cannot let her beat you, Princess. You must stop her from striking you."

"What can I do? If I resist, she will kill me. I have to go along with the cruelty until we are able to flee this place, my love." Cinderella's eighteenth birthday was in a fortnight. She had a plan to escape the castle, making her way to a new kingdom, where she could live in the woods with her love. The wolf snarled, hating the stepmother for her constant abuse of Cinderella. He wanted to be released into the castle so he could feast on the vile woman.

"Princess, this castle is your home. You should not be forced to flee from it living as a hag in the woods! We must develop a plan to remove your stepmother."

Cinderella shook her head. "No, my love...no more bloodshed. Nothing good ever came from vengeance. I will abdicate from my position as a princess and take refuge in a faraway land. The king has forgotten me. No one knows that princess Zezolla resides here. My days of royalty met their end the moment my father perished." Cinderella whimpered as she spoke, the sting of the Mugwort healing her wounds.

"What of your mother, my princess? What of the tree? You cannot abandon her."

Cinderella stroked her wolf as he nestled his head into her arm. "I will take a branch from the tree before burning it. In our new land, I will rebury the twig and call on mother's spirit to follow. She will come again to us, my love. She will always come to be with me as long as I have a twig of hazel to plant." Cinderella's eyes grew tired with sleep, the pain throbbing from her cuts. "Come lay by me, my love. I am too tired to speak of such things tonight."

The next day a royal messenger knocked on the castle door. Cinderella greeted the footman, bowing gracefully with her broom still in her hand.

"A royal message from the king himself." Said the footman. He handed Cinderella an invitation addressed to all the eligible maidens in the castle. The footman bowed as he took his leave and ventured on to the next home.

Jacqueline, Marguerite, Anastasia, and Drusilla all raced down the staircase, knocking each other over as they raced for Cinderella.

"Give it here!" Cried Jacqueline.

"Take your nasty hands off my letter, you wench!" Screamed Marguerite. The twins threw Cinderella to the ground as they snatched at the invitation, pushing their other sisters aside.

"LADIES!" Lady Tremaine bellowed as she made her way down the staircase; eyes burning red. The sisters stopped, forming a line. "Hand over the letter." Lady Tremaine seethed; her words were deadly. No love existed in her heart anymore – not even for her daughters. The loss of Claudette, her beautiful firstborn, had stripped her of any human kindness. The twins did as they were told, never looking their mother in the eye. Lady Tremaine now bore a cane, her grief aging her beyond her years.

"Well, there is to be a royal ball," announced Lady Tremaine.

"A ball!" Chimed her daughters excitedly.

"Yes, and it says by royal decree all eligible maidens are to attend." Cinderella stood up; her heart filled with hope. "The king is looking for a new queen. A young maiden who can bear him a child." Lady Tremaine paced back and forth ever so slowly as she read. "Whoever catches his eye at the ball will be declared the new queen of his kingdom and a ceremony will follow immediately." Lady Tremaine smirked with hope. "This, my daughters, will be your last attempt to make something of us! There are four of you left. You are not as pretty as your eldest sister, but you will have to do. If one of you does not catch the eye of the king, I will personally make you suffer the consequences." She stared at each of her daughters. "Do I make myself clear, my pets?"

The girls nodded, both fear and hope swelling in their hearts. "We have but three days before the ball. You will need to select your most gorgeous gowns, plan your hair styles, and practice your dancing. I cannot perform magic to make you shine out, so you will have to rely on your charm and wit to win the king's attention."

The girls held hands as images of the king soared through their minds. "Oh, to be queen," sighed Anastasia.

"Fat chance, sister." Said Drusilla. "The king will notice me! I shall be the queen." Drusilla swirled in a circle of delusion.

"Silence!" Lady Tremaine crashed her cane on the stone floor. "I do not care which one of you becomes queen just as long as one of you imbeciles makes it to the throne!"

The girls replied with a mechanical "yes, mother."

"Cinderella…" Lady Tremaine's voice was as cold as ice.

"Yes, Stepmother?"

"You will go with my daughters to their chambers and organize their gowns. Find their best and make them better. Do you understand?"

"Yes, stepmother."

The girls raced to their rooms, ordering Cinderella to follow. They tore through their wardrobes, throwing expensive gowns at Cinderella. "Not the blue one, the purple one, you idiot!" Yelled Marguerite. Cinderella dropped Marguerite's blue gown, picking up the purple one.

"She's so dim-witted. Are you sure the beast can even see colors?" Laughed Drusilla.

"Here, hexe. Take my dress and add pearls to it!" Marguerite threw her gown at Cinderella's face.

"What about me? I do not have anything to wear that will suit such a ball! Jacqueline, give me your red dress." Anastasia snatched her sister's dress out of her hands.

"Back off, you worm, this is to be my gown! Get one of your own pathetic dresses." She pushed Anastasia to the floor, clenching her gown. "I have chestnut brown hair. Red looks best on me!"

Anastasia pulled on her sister's leg, causing her to fall. "You little beast! How dare you?" Jacqueline whimpered.

Cinderella walked to the corner of the room, watching the amusing display before her.

Jacqueline yelled at her sister. "Stop it! We shouldn't be fighting amongst ourselves. It's her fault our dresses are not adequate!" She pointed to Cinderella. "Go find jewels to embellish our dresses!"

Cinderella looked at her stepsisters. "How? Where would I go to find jewels?"

Jacqueline slapped Cinderella across the face. "Don't talk back to me, servant! I am your master and I said to find us jewels! Steal them if you have to, I care not! Just don't return tonight without the jewels for our dresses!"

Cinderella cupped her face, staring at the fire. "As you wish, stepsister." She gathered the dresses and walked out of her sister's room.

"How is that filthy beast going to find us jewels? You shouldn't have sent her away, it's wasting time when she could be sewing our gowns." Marguerite crossed her arms, annoyed at her sister.

"She is a hexe, is she not? Let her grow the jewels from rocks for all I care." Hissed Jacqueline.

Cinderella returned to her cellar, setting the dresses down on a wooden chair. Her wolf walked over to her and licked her hand. "I do not know where I am going to find jewels, wolf. If I don't deliver their jewels by tonight, I will surely get another lashing." She sat in dismay whilst staring at the gowns.

"Princess, why don't you use some of the glass leaves from your mother's tree? They will do for jewels."

Cinderella praised her clever bird. "That is an excellent idea, my love!" She stood up, instantly racing out of the cellar. "Come wolf. Come join us for a stroll in the forest."

Cinderella came to her mother's tree. She reached for a branch, plucking off one of the radiant leaves. "My daughter, why must you take a leaf from my branch?"

"Mother, there is to be a royal ball where the king will select a queen. My stepsister Jacqueline ordered me to gather jewels for her dress. I do not own any, so I thought I could trick her with one of your lovely glass leaves." The tree did not reply as it retracted its branches from Cinderella's reach. "Mother, what is it?"

"A ball, you say? I'll tell you what, my lovely daughter. I will give you some of my glass leaves, but

106

only for your stepsister Jacqueline." Cinderella listened as her mother struck a deal. "If I do this for you, my daughter, you must agree to go to the ball as well."

Cinderella laughed. "Mother, that is not possible! I do not own a dress. Even if I did, my stepmother would never allow me to attend."

The tree lowered its branches to Cinderella, allowing her to gather a few of the brilliant leaves. "Let that be for me to worry about, my daughter. Take your leaves and sew them into the bust of your stepsister's dress." Cinderella collected six glass leaves, thanking her mother for the gift. "Remember, Daughter. You must sew them into the bust of only Jacqueline's gown."

"Yes, mother. I will." Cinderella turned to leave the forest but stopped as she heard her mother's voice call out to her.

"Leave the wolf with me. I have a favor to ask of him."

Cinderella turned to her wolf, kissing him on the head. "Stay here, my pet. I will return shortly."

Cinderella worked diligently throughout the day on her stepsisters dresses. As instructed by her mother, she sewed the glass leaves into the bust of Jacquelines. "It will truly be a beautiful gown, my love. The king will surely notice her with these glass leaves." The raven sat in silence as he watched Cinderella hard at work. She used vines from the garden as thread, fastening the glass to the bust. "It looks like a dress suitable for a fairy." Cinderella smiled happily at her accomplishment.

"Truly the loveliest gown I have seen, my princess. You have outdone yourself."

Cinderella stroked her raven's head. "Let us hope my stepsister agrees, my love." The moon crept through the castle halls as Cinderella made her way to Jacqueline's room. She knocked on the door before entering. "Stepsister, I have completed your dress."

Jacqueline sat on her bed, sucking on a piece of chocolate as Cinderella entered. "It's so creamy and decadent. They call it chocolate. Have you ever had one before?"

Cinderella replied with a yes, when she was young-too young to clearly remember the delicious taste.

"Maybe if I'm pleased with my dress, I will give you one." She cocked her head to Cinderella, her voice velvety and kind. "Would you like that, dear stepsister?"

Cinderella, not being a naive soul, only replied with, "if it pleases you, stepsister, then it would please me." Cinderella placed the dress on the bed, fanning out the delicate fabric.

Jacqueline traced her hand along the silk. "It's magnificent! Jeweled leaves! Where did you find such expensive and rare jewels?"

Cinderella shrugged her shoulders. "I came upon them in the forest. It was serendipity."

Jacqueline laughed, lifting up the gown. "Serendipity indeed, hexe." She ordered for Cinderella to dress her. "This shall be the gown to win the king's attention. You did well."

Jacqueline admired her reflection in the mirror. The gown was in fact exquisite, and she would never have another that was its equal. She walked back to her box of chocolates. "Only one remaining." She picked up the sweet, handing it to her stepsister. Cinderella kept her hands by her side. Jacqueline snarled, popping the chocolate in her mouth. "Oh, it's so creamy." She closed her eyes, savoring the flavor. "I should have known you wouldn't trust me. Of course, I would never bestow an act of kindness upon you. Not even a simple, tiny chocolate." Jacqueline twirled in circles, the sparkling leaves casting a soft glow like rays of sunshine across the room. "Leave me, Cinderella. Your ugliness is ruining the elegance of my gown."

Cinderella bowed, exiting the room as Jacqueline called for her other sisters to come and see her new treasure.

Anastasia growled with greed. "Where's mine? Why didn't that beast make me one with jeweled leaves?"

Jacqueline laughed at her sorry sister. "She has only found enough for one dress, my dress. The dress that will shine out amongst the rest at the ball!"

Lady Tremaine entered the room, overhearing the commotion. "What is all this ruckus about?" She stopped, eyeing her second eldest in the gorgeous gown. "Oh, Jacqueline, that dress! It will shine above all the rest at the ball." The other sisters moved closer, jealousy coursing through their veins as they became overcome with greed. "It's not fair! Why does she get a gown like that and we don't?" Whined the twins.

Their mother struck each girl in the leg with her cane. "Silence! If one of you succeed, then all of us benefit! It is apparent that Jacqueline will be the one to win the king's favor and become queen." She placed her hand on her mouth, delighted at the thought of seeing Jacqueline sitting on the throne. "All my hard work will pay off." Her eyes drifting into a dreamy state. She was unaware as Marguerite crept upon her sister; fists clenched.

Marguerite touched the vine on her sister's dress. "She used real vines to attach the leaves." Her voice low and harsh.

"Admire away, my pathetic sister, for you will never own a gown such as this."

Marguerite touched one of the leaves that hovered over her sister's heart. Thoughts of murder entered her mind, images of the jewel leaf striking her sister through the heart. Her hand trembled as her hatred grew. She did not hear her mother screaming as she stood before her sister. Jacqueline's eyes closed, blood pouring from her chest. Lady Tremaine pushed Marguerite to the floor, frantically ripping the gown off her daughter. Marguerite glanced at her hand, noticing a thick coat of crimson blood pooling out of her blue-green veins. "What? What has happened?"

Lady Tremaine screamed in horror at the glass leaf lodged in her daughter's heart.

She turned on Marguerite, grabbing her in rage. "You killed her! You killed your sister!"

Marguerite cried in terror, never meaning to go through with the macabre thoughts that had raced through her mind. "I didn't mean to! I don't know how I did that! I… I…I just wanted the dress to be mine."

Her mother picked up her cane and struck her daughter over the shoulder with it. "My two eldest daughters are gone! Payment for the blood shed I have caused on others. You are my last hope for a future. Get up and collect yourself! The ball is in two nights and I will not have your faces swollen and ugly for the king." Lady Tremaine glared at her remaining daughters. "Find Cinderella. Have her sew your gowns. I need you looking your best."

Anastasia and Drusilla ran to their sister, helping her to her feet. "What do we do with the body? Do we bury her?" Drusilla trembled as she looked upon her dead sister's face. "Should we shut her eyes?"

Marguerite used two fingers to close Jacqueline's eyes. "I never meant to kill her." Her voice was barely audible.

Anastasia rang the servant's bell, summoning Cinderella. "Let Hexe dispose of the body." Decided Anastasia.

Cinderella entered her stepsister's room, shocked by the body lying motionless on the floor. "What happened?"

Marguerite charged at Cinderella, grabbing her by the hair. "Look what you did! This is all your fault! Your cursed jewels killed our sister, stabbing her through the heart!" Cinderella saw the glass leaf sticking out of Jacqueline's chest. "You are the reason our sister is gone. Take her body and bury it in the garden!"

Cinderella knelt beside her dead stepsister, unable to comprehend the event which took place. She glanced up at her remaining stepsisters. "How am I to carry her alone?"

"Not our problem, beasty!" Screamed Drusilla. "Figure it out!" The sisters headed back to their rooms, but as she left Marguerite called out, "and when you are done, prepare our gowns. No magic this time, hexe, or I will bury you next to my dead sister."

Cinderella dragged Jacqueline through the castle, making her way into the garden. "Come to me, my love!"

Her black raven came to her side. "What has happened, princess?"

"My mother. She must have cursed the leaves, so they would plunge into her heart when they were touched."

The raven agreed. "That's why she instructed you to sew the glass leaves into the bust. So they would be near her heart."

Cinderella went to the shed, selecting a shovel. "I am to bury her."

"Why should you bury their dead when they have never done anything for you?"

"There is no one else to bury her and she deserves a resting place."

The raven snorted. "This girl was pure evil. She deserves to roam the night in eternal darkness, never feeling any peace."

"Hush, my love." Cinderella looked at the body. "Everyone deserves eternal peace." The raven flew off into the night, leaving his princess to dig the grave.

Cinderella paused, exhaustion and pain taking over her limbs. Her back was still not fully healed and digging such a deep hole was too hard on the girl. She sat down next to her stepsister's body, wishing she could end all this death. Two blue eyes glowed at the edge of the forest. "Who's there? Wolf, is that you, my pet?" The wolf ran over to his mistress, gently nudging her with his nose. "I'm just resting, my pet. Once I have the strength, I will continue to dig this grave." She looked out into the forest. More eyes shone brightly in the night. "Are there others with you, wolf?" The wolf raised his head, releasing a howl into the sky. Cinderella stood up as a pack of wolves made their way to her. "Are they friends or enemies, my pet?"

Her wolf bit into Jacqueline's shoulder, dragging her limp body across the earth. "What are you doing, my pet?" He placed Jacqueline between Cinderella and the incoming wolves.

"Princess, you must return to the castle. Hurry! Go inside now," instructed her raven.

"My love, what is happening?"

"They have fresh meat. Leave before they become crazed by human blood. Come! You must leave. Now!"

Cinderella ran, following her raven to the castle, leaving the sounds of snarling and the tearing of flesh behind her.

In Preparation

Cinderella awoke the next morning covered in dirt with her raven and her wolf by her side. "You saved me last night, wolf".

He licked her hand, laying his head upon her. "You didn't take any flesh from my stepsister, did you? There is no trace of blood in your mouth." Again, the wolf licked her hand. Cinderella got up, collecting her stepsisters dresses. "I have one day to complete three dresses before the ball tomorrow. How will I manage with all my other chores?" She looked to her raven for advice.

"CINDERELLA!"

Screams from the castle roared down the cellar.

"They never venture this far down the castle. I will have to work on these dresses tonight."

The raven was disgusted by the stepsisters. He wanted to shred the dresses into pieces and leave them unable to attend the ball, but that would only bring his beloved harm. "I must figure out a way to help the princess. She will never have enough time to turn these dresses into gowns by tomorrow." He looked over at the wolf. "Any suggestions, friend?" The wolf stared back; a blank expression on his face.

Cinderella was ordered to shine her stepsister's shoes and bathe, wash, and curl each girl's hair. Even her stepmother required special pampering. Cinderella worked as quickly as she could, but the night sky was quickly approaching. She feared what would become of her if she could not finish the dresses in time. Cinderella washed her stepmother's hair as Lucifer sat on the edge of the tub, purring at his mistress. Lady Tremaine had long, dark hair with streaks of grey trailing along the back.

"Wash it slowly, you ungraceful beast."

Cinderella carefully separated the hair into even strands, washing each one at a time. "You will have to set my hair tonight so it will be ready for the ball."

"Yes, stepmother." Cinderella reached for rose oil and massaged it into her stepmother's scalp.

"You were a lovely child, Cinderella."

Cinderella stopped, frozen by the comment.

"Well? What do you say to someone who pays you a compliment, child?"

"Thank you, stepmother."

"I had taught you better than that, Cinderella. I will not tolerate rudeness."

"Yes, of course, stepmother; my apologies."

"You had a sweet disposition to you, always seeking approval from those you wanted love from. You adored me, of course. You saw me as your savior. A safe haven when your whore of a mother was too busy destroying your future. If only that stupid woman played it safer, she would still be alive."

Cinderella blinked back her tears. Memories of her mother's death still haunted her. The spirit of her mother could never replace the warm body she craved. The hazel tree was only the ghost of her mother.

Lady Tremaine reached for Cinderella, pulling her forward. "You are almost eighteen. Tomorrow is your birthday. Is it not?"

"Yes, stepmother."

"Hmm… a lady then you will be when you awake."

"I suppose so, stepmother."

"Do not mistake your age for nobility. You may be a lady by years, but you are a servant by rank and always will be."

"Yes, stepmother."

"When Marguerite marries the king, we will be moving into the Royal Castle. I suppose you think I will depart from this castle and hand it over to you?"

"No, my stepmother, I do not anticipate that at all."

"Ha! Clever girl, of course I would never leave you my castle. I will keep it shut down and boarded up tight so that no one will ever be able to occupy its halls." She glanced sideways at Cinderella. "You will be homeless."

"Yes, stepmother, I suppose I will be."

"No one to love, care, or support you. You will end up in a brothel, most likely."

Cinderella hid her anger behind her stoic face in which she shielded herself with. "Unless… I might find the kindness in my heart, to bring you to the Royal Castle along with us as the hog tender. You do love animals. You can sleep with the pigs in their sty where you will feed, wash, and care for them." She smiled at Cinderella. "How does that sound, my stepdaughter? Princess of the Swine?"

Cinderella bowed her head. "It would suit me fine. You are too generous, stepmother."

"Yes...I am. Now finish my bath. You have other duties before the sun sets and I will not tolerate laziness."

The stepsisters kept Cinderella busy into the early hours of her eighteenth birthday. She left their chambers exhausted, weak from work, and covered in soot. She did not wish to go to the tree that evening. She had other matters on her mind. If indeed her stepsister became queen, Cinderella would be cast into the streets. She knew her stepmother would never bring her to the castle, not even as the swine herder. It would be too risky for Lady Tremaine if someone discovered her true identity, as that would pose a threat to her stepmother. Cinderella knew that she would need to flee the castle tomorrow evening when her stepsisters left for the ball.

When Cinderella entered the cellar, she saw three beautiful gowns hanging on the wall. She called for her raven. "My love, come to me."

The bird appeared, bowing. "A gift for you, my princess." Cinderella held out her arm for her bird. He gladly perched upon her, rubbing his head against her fair skin.

"My love? Where did you get these dresses?"

The raven looked lovingly at his princess. "I took them from a traveling merchant. He won't notice their absence."

"You stole them so I wouldn't get beaten?"

"Yes, my princess. You would never have been able to sew these dresses in time for the ball tomorrow night, and besides, I wanted to give you a birthday present, even if it is just these dresses for your evil stepsisters."

Cinderella loved her raven; his loyalty and devotion to her was gift enough. "No one has ever shown me such kindness and adoration. Thank you, my love" she said as she kissed his head. "I do not deserve you."

"You deserve the world Princess. I am sorry I am but a raven and not a man who can give you more."

Cinderella laughed at the thought of a human man being kinder than her raven. "No, my love, a man could never love me as you do. I have seen into the hearts of men and they are flawed. But not yours, my raven, your heart is pure and everlasting." Cinderella looked at the moon. "The sun will be rising in a few hours. I must go to the tree before bed. Will you come with me, my love?"

The raven accompanied his princess through the forest. Only the sound of his wings filled the silent sky. Her wolf was waiting for her. "Hello, my pet. I see you've found a comfortable spot to rest." He was nestled under the tree, lying on a bed of moss. The wolf greeted Cinderella with a bow.

"Mother, I need to ask a question of you."

"What troubles you, my daughter?"

"Did you curse the leaves you gave me? My stepsister is dead."

"Yes. She did not deserve such a gown made from my glass leaves. She got the ending that she deserved."

Cinderella looked at the ground with pure shame in her heart. "I do not wish my step-sisters dead. They are cruel and terribly wicked, but death is not a method for revenge."

The tree shook its branches, shedding its glass leaves. "It is the way I seek justice. You are innocent of all blood spilled."

"Promise me no more death will come to my stepsisters by your doing?"

The tree shook again. "If that is your wish."

"It is, mother."

"So it shall be."

Cinderella touched one of the branches, caressing it as if it were her mother's own arm.

"Mother, tomorrow is the ball. If one of my step-sisters catch the eye of the king, I will be thrown out without a home. I plan on leaving when they depart for the ball. I cannot stay here any longer."

"I understand, my daughter. But now it is you who must promise me something."

"Anything, mother."

"When the sun sets and the sisters leave in their carriage, you must come straight here to say your goodbyes. Do not pack. Do not collect any of your things."

Cinderella thought that was a curious request. "Of course, mother. I shall come immediately."

The tree was pleased with Cinderella's response. "Thank you, daughter. Now go and collect some sleep. You will need your rest for the day ahead."

"Goodnight, mother."

"Until tomorrow, my daughter. Happy birthday."

To Be Broken

The day of the ball was hectic for Cinderella. She was jostled around by her stepsisters, unable to keep up with their constant demands.

"Hurry up, lazy! I said I needed my hair pinned back in flowers! What is taking you so long?"

"Coming, Drusilla. I'm finishing Anastasia's nails."

"To hell with my sister! I said now!"

"You shut up, Drusilla! Wait your turn!"

"Cinderella!" Marguerite hollered from across the hall. "I need my stockings dried!"

Cinderella did her best to complete all their demands but was failing to do so. "Cinderella. You are to meet the needs of all my daughters. Get moving or I will unleash one hell of a lashing upon you." Lady Tremaine entered Drusilla's room with her cane in hand.

"Yes, stepmother." She hurried to Drusilla, pinning the flowers into her bun. She ran to Marguerite, ironing her stockings dry. She tried to be diligent, but still her stepsisters barked more orders at her. She fastened the pearls around one stepsister's neck while hanging beaded earrings in another. Her stepmother watched over her with an evil eye the entire time. Cinderella crushed some berries for lipstick with the screams of the sisters echoing behind her. Cinderella's hands were shaking. She couldn't move any faster. As she approached Marguerite, she tripped over her stepmother's cane.

"Clumsy fool!" Yelled Lady Tremaine. Her stepmother lashed at her back, tearing through her dress. Again, and again her stepmother's cane came down upon her flesh. Unable to move from exhaustion, Cinderella begged her stepmother to stop.

"Please, stepmother! I cannot prepare your daughters for the ball if you beat me!"

A fire ignited in Lady Tremaine. "Did you dare speak back to me?"

"Please! I can't take any more lashings. I won't be able to walk if you continue to beat me."

"You cannot walk anyway, you clumsy witch!" She backed up, restraining her cane. "Get up, you useless soul."

Cinderella tried to stand, but her knees gave out. The pain was too intense for her to move.

Anastasia took a handful of berries and smeared them in Cinderella's face. "You heard my mother. Get up!"

Cinderella tried to rise and placed her weight on her hand, but once more she collapsed.

Drusilla grabbed a broom and began sweeping Cinderella in the face. "Get up, you filth! Get moving!"

The girls were laughing as they each took their turn at mocking their stepsister. Marguerite scooped a cup of ash from the fireplace. "Open her mouth, Drusilla." Anastasia held Cinderella down, pressing on her fresh wounds. Cinderella cried out in pain, unable to fight back. Drusilla pried Cinderella's mouth open as Marguerite emptied ash and soot into her mouth. Cinderella gagged, choking. Her mouth filled with soot; her tongue caked in ash.

"Girls...girls...we don't want to murder the poor beast, just torment her." Said Lady Tremaine. She looked at the sun setting in the purple and orange sky. "That is enough fun, ladies. We have grander plans for tonight. It is time we depart for the ball."

The girls stepped over Cinderella's broken body; each kicking her in the ribs. "Goodnight Cinderella and happy birthday" sang Marguerite.

Cinderella lay on the ground, utterly defeated. She was sure her back was broken. Tears began to streak down her cheeks. She tried to crawl to the hall but was unable to do so. "My love...come to me." She called out to her raven hoping, he could hear her feeble cry.

"My princess!" He swooped down, scooping out the ash in his princess's mouth. "I can't move. She broke my back."

The raven cried in agony. "I will kill that woman! I will pluck her eyes from their sockets!"

Cinderella looked at the blood beside her. She knew her injuries were great. "My raven, I cannot move. What am I to do?"

"Don't worry, my princess. I will get help!" He flew out of the window, flying with a vengeance. He raced against the wind, not stopping until he made his way to the tree. "My lady! My princess is hurt! Lady Tremaine beat her, and I fear she may die. She is bleeding from the inside."

"Come here, wolf!" commanded the tree. "My daughter requires help. Go to her. Place her on your shoulders and carry her to me." The tree stretched out its branches, casting a silver mist upon the wolf. The mist raised the wolf in the air, encircling his body. "Where there were once paws, let there be hooves! Where there once was fur, let there be a mane! Where there was once a wolf, let there be a horse!" The mother's words made the ground tremble, lifting the wolf higher and higher into the air, his body morphing into a stallion.

The mist lowered the horse to the ground. "Now go quickly! Bring me my daughter! She hasn't much time!"

The horse ran beside the raven as they bolted toward the castle. The earth shook as each of the horse's hooves stomped on the ground.

"The castle door is locked, my friend, you must kick it in" the raven commanded.

The horse raised his front legs, fiercely breaking down the wooden door. He mounted the stairs, following the raven to his mistress. Cinderella lay immobile on the stone floor, her eyes cloudy and tainted black by the ash trapped inside. "Hurry, wolf! Lower your body so she may climb on." The wolf lowered his new form and nudged Cinderella onto his shoulders. The raven took a bit of ribbon and wrapped it around Cinderella's body, attaching it to the horse.

"Run, wolf! Run hard back to the tree!"

The Grand Ball

Cinderella was unconscious as the tree gingerly picked her up, cradling her in its branches. "Raven, a sacrifice must be made to save my daughter." The raven flew to Cinderella placing his beak on her face.

"If there is a sacrifice to be made, let it be from me." He looked upon his princess with an ache in his heart for he would never see her beautiful face again. "I love you, my princess. I have always loved you and I will continue to love you, even in death." He flew back to the ground bowing to the tree. "I am ready." The tree took one of its branches and stabbed the raven with a glass leaf.

"From the end of this raven bring a new beginning for my daughter. From the ashes of sorrow bring forth the gift of life!"

Cinderella gasped, life entering her lungs. She blinked away the ash from her eyes and felt the sting of pain leaving her body. She cuddled the branches, relieved to be alive. "Mother, you saved me." The tree placed Cinderella softly on the ground laying her next to the dead raven. Cinderella reached for her bird before realizing he was no more. "No! No! Wake up, my love! Wake up!" She pulled the bird into her arms crying frantically into his wings.

"What have you done?" She screamed at the tree backing away from it.

"It had to be done, my daughter. I did not wish the raven to die, but a sacrifice was required to save you. I was fond of your raven and this is not something I wanted. I am sorry."

"No! Not my love!"

"He gave his life for yours because he loved you. He wanted you to continue on."

"I have no reason to live without him. He was all I had."

"You are a princess. Do not forget who you are! You must go on and you must seek your rightful place on the throne."

"There is no throne, Mother! I am a servant! No one knows or remembers me as Princess Zezolla. I have become Cinderella!"

"Never! You will not continue on as a servant. I gave birth to a princess not a slave! You will attend the ball tonight and you will enchant the king!"

Cinderella shook her head. "The ball? No! Why would I go to the ball? I am no one!"

"You are my daughter. The daughter of Prince Baldric of Munich and you are no commoner!"

"I have no gown, no carriage, and I have no shoes! How could I ever attend the ball?"

The tree spun its branches casting a white glow over Cinderella. She looked at her body, her rags falling to the ground.

"Stand, my daughter."

Cinderella kissed her bird placing him carefully on a bed of moss. She stood naked before the hazel tree.

"From my branches to your body, don my daughter in a gown of silver." Light extended from the branches covering Cinderella. "Twirl, my daughter, twirl around and around." Cinderella twirled, the light spinning over her wrapping its glow around her tiny frame. When she came to a stop, she was not naked, but clothed in the most exquisite gown spun from pure silver. She gasped at the magnificence of the dress.

"It's stunning, Mother. It's the most gorgeous gown I have ever seen."

"Take two of my leaves, Daughter." Cinderella plucked two leaves from the tree. "Place them on the ground." Cinderella did as her mother instructed placing the leaves in front of her feet. "Step on them, my daughter." Cinderella took her right foot and moved it on top of the leaf then her left on the other. "From the leaves of my sorrow to the journey of my daughter. Serve her well, glass slippers."

Cinderella lifted her gown raising her foot in the air. "Glass slippers! Mother, I've never seen their equal!"

"Nor shall you ever, my daughter."

"But Mother, I still do not have a carriage."

"You have a steed instead."

Cinderella turned to the gray horse. "Blue eyes. I know those eyes." She cupped the horse's face placing her head upon his. "My pet, is that you?"

The wolf nodded and she clung tightly. "Thank you for saving my life, my pet." Her eyes filled with tears. "If only my raven didn't have to die." She picked up her bird, took a branch from the hazel tree, and did a bit of her own magic. "From what was mine, but was taken, please protect my love until he can be awakened." The branch formed into a small wooden coffin and she placed her bird inside closing the glass lid.

"Please watch over my raven until I return, Mother."

"I will guard him well, my daughter. You have my word."

Cinderella turned to her horse noticing she needed a saddle. She spun around looking for something she could use in another spell. An apple tree sat close by. She twisted an apple off a branch and placed it on the horse.

"From fruit to saddle make me a seat." Cinderella, pleased with her own magic, walked over to her mother's tree. "Mother? What of my face? My stepmother and stepsisters will notice me, and they will sabotage my chances with the king."

"Take a piece of ivy which climbs up my trunk and place it around your neck." Cinderella took the ivy and tied it a knot. "Vine of the earth, blind those who mean to harm my daughter and let her face go unseen."

Cinderella felt the vine tighten around her neck turning into a beautiful sage green choker, her knot transforming into a solid clasp. Cinderella mounted her horse grabbing his mane.

"Remember, my daughter. As with all magic, time is of the essence. You must return by the stroke of midnight. The vine can only protect you from harm until midnight when my magic will weaken and everything that is will be as it was."

"I understand Mother."

Cinderella rode to the castle staying clear of the main roads. She didn't want anyone to notice her presence. "Bring me to that edge of that clearing, my pet, but no further." The castle was still a way off, but Cinderella preferred to walk to the castle gate rather than arrive on horseback. "Stay here, my pet. I will be back before midnight." She kissed the horse and made her way through the castle's courtyard.

Guards in blue and white velvet lined the entrance and each held a sword in their hands. As Cinderella approached the castle stairs, she considered turning back. She did not want the life of a queen married to a king she could never love. She longed for her raven and the future that was stolen from them.

"My lady." A guard came to collect Cinderella's hand escorting her into the castle. "You must be acknowledged upon entering the ball. What house are you from, my lady?" asked the guard.

Cinderella didn't hesitate to answer. "Raven. I am The Lady of the House of Raven."

"Very good, my lady." The guard placed Cinderella's hand around his arm as he led her to the ballroom. She looked at the crystal chandeliers, remembering her life back in Munich. She was once the princess of a royal castle. She lived in luxury, never lifting a finger. Everything she could ever desire was at her disposal. Oddly, she did not long for those days. She felt pity for the royals for they had no understanding of what it meant to do a hard days work . Each night when nobles closed their eyes, they are not welcoming sleep in exhaustion from a day of work. They do not know the privilege of feeling grateful to have an hour extra of rest. To Cinderella, each day she awoke alive and healthy was a blessing. Every time she walked with her raven and watched him soar into the clouds was a moment of freedom. Royals could never comprehend such emotion, and for that, Cinderella felt blessed.

"May I present The Lady of the House of Raven." announced the guard. The ball came to a halt as all eyes fell on Cinderella. She curtsied politely and headed into the crowd. Men and women made a path for the beautiful lady as she took her place on the dance floor. Gentlemen had already lined up to dance with her.

She graciously accepted the hand of a wealthy noble. "You are truly exquisite, my lady. I have never seen such a beauty in all the lands."

"You are very kind, young sir." Cinderella twirled around the dance floor, oblivious that everyone intensely watched her every move. She danced into the night accepting the hand of more noblemen who were all enchanted by her black hair, fair skin, and blue eyes. Whispers spread fast of The Lady of the House of Raven and her beauty traveled across the lips of all the guests.

"Her hair is as black as a raven and her eyes are as blue as ice." whispered a woman.

"Did you notice her gown? Pure silver! It's divine!" gossiped another.

"I heard she comes from the North, the daughter of a wealthy king!" added a man.

Cinderella enjoyed the praise and attention. She found it odd that people might see her as beautiful when she spent her days donned in rags, covered in ash and soot. She roamed the ball drifting from one admirer to the next, but secretly she was searching for her stepmother and stepsisters. She was terrified that the spell on her choker wouldn't conceal her identity and all would be ruined once they recognized her.

Exhausted from dancing, Cinderella wandered to the balcony for some solitude and fresh air. She was overwhelmed by all the people surrounding her. Isolation had been such an imperative part of her life and she had learned to truly love being forever alone with only her raven. Their bond had created a deep connection, a connection someone could not form by spending their days surrounded by the mindless chatter of too many people. Unlike others, all Cinderella needed was one. One person to love and in return be loved by them. Cinderella grew up not relying on people for support or emotional comfort. Her animals were her companions and her magic sustained her by supplying her with endless pleasure. She looked at the faces in the ballroom through the glass door. Mindless statues gossiping and backstabbing one another. Cinderella felt tired and wanted to return to her horse, back to her tree, and to sit in the moonlight with her departed raven.

Voices were coming from the south wing of the balcony and she saw the king approaching with

Marguerite on his arm. Cinderella dashed behind a column, praying she would go unnoticed. She peeked around the corner observing the two. The king was listening as Marguerite told him of her passion for the arts. The king looked behind them as Anastasia, Drusilla, and Lady Tremaine followed.

"Do your mother and sisters always accompany you when you go for a stroll?"

Marguerite laughed, waving her hand in the air. "Oh, they are just curious. It's not every day you get to be in the company of such a powerful and handsome king."

The King half smiled clearly unamused by Marguerite's compliments. The King came to a stop as his head guard approached. "Your Majesty. If I may have a private word?"

"Of course." The king kissed Marguerite's hand. "If you will excuse me."

Marguerite waved as the king walked out of sight. "He's so dreamy! And he's quite fond of me!" She fell into Anastasia's arms, too weak from excitement to stand.

"You are so lucky! What does he feel like?"

"That's the stupidest question, Anastasia."

Drusilla spoke up. "What does he smell like?"

Anastasia's face lit up. "Oh, what does he smell like!? I've never smelled a king before."

Marguerite laughed at her sisters. "Oh, you two are so simple! No wonder the king selected me. He sensed my maturity and worldliness."

Lady Tremaine walked closer to her daughter. "Do not get overly confident yet, my daughter. You have done

132

well detaining him this far into the night, but whispers are circling of a rare beauty. A maiden from The House of Raven."

"I've never heard of her?" Marguerite became concerned.

"It's nothing to fret over, Marguerite. Just keep the king by your side and away from the ball. We don't want him to run into this mysterious maiden and ruin our chances of you becoming queen."

Cinderella clenched her chest, "They will destroy me if they discover I am the maiden they worry over. I have to leave. I can't risk them discovering my true identity." She waited for her stepsisters and stepmother to leave the balcony, wondering after the king. Cinderella took the stone steps leading to the garden, her feet not moving fast enough. She paused as she heard the king talking to his guard.

"I could not love her, but she will suffice as a wife. She is educated, attractive, and young enough to bear children."

"You have selected then, my king?"

"Yes, I suppose I have. Do not make the announcement until the end of the ball."

"Of course, my King."

Cinderella's heart was crushed. Not because she would never be queen, but because one of the most wicked women in the land was now going to rule by the side of the king. If Marguerite and her stepsisters revel in such immense pleasure in being cruel to only one person, what will they do when they have true power over the entire kingdom? She decided to leave that night. She would ride her horse into a new land finding refuge in the forest, living out her days as a solitary witch with her animals. She would not stay in a land where such an evil ruled over the innocent.

It Comes Undone

"My lady, where are you going?"

Cinderella froze. She knew that voice. It belonged to the king. She quickly regrouped herself. "Your Majesty." She delicately curtsied; her silver gown sparkling in the night sky.

The king was mesmerized by the woman before him. He moved closer to her staring into her blue eyes. "Your hair is black as night."

"As ravens' wings my king." She wondered if she had said too much and if that would give away her identity as The Princess Zezolla, the little girl he met beside a grave. She waited for a reply, any sign, or indication that he remembered her. Cinderella searched his face wanting to believe that he did not forget about the little princess who was left to rot in a castle.

"Ravens' wings…Ah. You must be The Lady of the House of Raven." He took her hand kissing it. Cinderella hid her disappointment behind a smile. He did forget her. In all these years his thoughts never once ventured to the orphan child who was once a princess.

"Yes Your Majesty. I am she."

"I have heard whispers all evening of your beauty, but I thought they were just rumors for I have never seen a woman with black hair who could make a king weak in the knees until now."

"My king, you flatter me so."

"Were you departing just now? Why would you leave before the naming of my bride to be?" The king looked into the grounds, curious what a lovely maiden would be doing at night all alone in the courtyard.

"No, I was not leaving Your Majesty. Why, I had not met you yet and why would I ever leave a royal ball without meeting the handsome king?"

He laughed at her comment, amused by her charm and wit. "Would you care to walk with me under the moonlight then, my lady?"

Cinderella took his arm and strolled along the grounds. She did admire the immense beauty of the castle. It was enchanting. They came upon a bridge and Cinderella leaned over the side staring at the moon's reflection in the water. "It's extremely lovely here, Your Majesty. Thank you for showing me your enchanting gardens."

He turned Cinderella around placing his hands around her waist. "You like it here then, my lady."

"Very much, Your Majesty."

"Would you like to stay here?"

Cinderella bit her bottom lip. No. No, she wouldn't want to stay there. Not with a king detested for neglecting her. Not with a prison disguised as a castle to enslave her into another life, a life of childbearing. But these things she could not admit to the king.

"You do not respond? You are unlike the other maidens. Shyer and more modest." He pulled Cinderella closer brushing her hair with his hand. "I think you would like to stay here. I think you would make a fine queen."

Cinderella's heart quickened. *No! No, I don't want this. I must get out of here now!* Her thoughts screamed into her head. She had to think of a way to escape from the king's romantic advances. She looked around her. What could she use to summon someone? She saw a lily pad with a frog sitting on it. She whispered softly, "Find a stepsister and bring her to the king." Away the frog hopped heading to the castle. Cinderella knew the frog would return with Marguerite. She would have to hold off the king's advances until she arrived.

"A queen? Your Majesty, you honour me so. Imagine me as your queen." She laughed at her own words.

"It is not flattery, my lady. It is my wish."

Cinderella tried to pull away, but the King's grip was tight. "Do not leave me for the night, my lady. You are to be my queen. It will be announced tonight. Tomorrow at first light I will send for your family at the House of Raven. We shall have our wedding the next day and you will be my queen." He pulled Cinderella close to him, kissing her passionately and without her consent. She hated his lips, hated his taste – she did not want his body pressed up against hers. She tried to resist, but he was more powerful. She pushed her hands against his chest, but he pinned them behind her back. He paused only for a moment to whisper into her ear.

"You have bewitched not only my mind, but also my soul. I will not let you leave. Not now; not ever."

Anxiety arose in Cinderella. She felt trapped. Closed in as if she were suffocating. She mentally willed Marguerite to appear. She willed it so intensely that voices were heard across the garden. The king's grasp loosened. "Who is approaching?" He was annoyed by the disturbance.

"Looks like some of your subjects, Your Majesty."

He called to his guards. "Take care of those meddling women. I do not want any interruptions while I'm with my lady." Cinderella saw her opportunity to escape.

Thankfully in this case, Lady Tremaine would not be dismissed so easily. She walked past the guards ignoring their demands. "I will see the king. He has been with my daughter all evening and we will not be ignored."

Marguerite looked coldly at the unknown woman standing beside the king. "Mother! Why is he with her?"

"Hush girl. Just follow my lead." Lady Tremaine curtsied. "Your Majesty. There is a restlessness stirring in the castle."

"What manner of issue could there be?" asked the king coldly.

"Your guests are requesting a dance in your honor. They are growing uneasy without your presence."

Cinderella held her breath, hoping her identity would not be recognized. Her stepmother came closer to the king, glancing over at the lady to his right. "My lady," she said to Cinderella. Cold chills tingled down Cinderella's spine. Her stepmother had not noticed her face. The enchanted vine had worked.

The King waved his hand in the air. "Very well, I shall return to the ball. I have an announcement to make anyway." He reached for Cinderella's arm. She reluctantly accepted, thoughts of escape occupying her mind. Marguerite began to follow the king as they made their way to the castle. Her face burning with jealousy. Lady Tremaine held out her cane, tripping her daughter.

The King let go of Cinderella rushing to the fallen maiden. "Careful, my lady."

Marguerite seized the opportunity before her. "Oh, my King, I believe I have twisted my ankle."

He bent down inspecting her injury. His strong hands roamed over her leg, searching for the injury. "It might be a sprain. Come. I'll help you to the castle."

Cinderella quietly backed into the night, using the cover of darkness to conceal herself. Marguerite leaned against the King feigning whimpers as she tried to take a step. Cinderella ran to the other end of the bridge. She crawled to the lake hiding in the water.

When the king looked for his maiden, he was angry to notice her gone. "Where is the lady I was just with?"

Lady Tremaine looked behind them. "Lady, my king?"

"Yes! The lady who was just with me. Where did she go?"

"I do not know, my king. Perhaps back to the castle."

The king ordered his guards to search the ground. "Find the Lady of the House of Raven. Bring her to me at once!"

The guards looked at each other. "My king, what did she look like?" they asked.

The king ran his hand through his hair. "She…she has…her hair was…" The king could not remember what the lady's features were like. "She was just here! Did you not notice her?"

The guards looked at each other unsure of a proper response. "We did see her, my King, but we cannot remember what she looked like."

The King turned to Lady Tremaine, irritated. "You saw her. Tell them of her looks!"

Lady Tremaine was perplexed for she herself could not recall the features of the woman who was just before them. "I do not remember her appearance, my King."

The King began to get violent. "It was just moments ago! How is this possible? Spread out! I want her found!"

The guards knew better than to speak up. They began to search for a lady whom no one could describe. The King was irritated by his men. He began to search the bridge; frustration taking over. "How can no one recall the lady's face? She had a silver dress with glass slippers. Find any maiden with glass slippers and bring them to me."

The Fitting of the Glass Slipper

Cinderella waited until the guards moved from the bridge. She crouched down low allowing the water to conceal her dress and body. All that was exposed were her blue eyes and black hair. She held her breath willing her lungs to keep breathing without oxygen. She couldn't risk coming up for a breath and being seen. When her lungs could no longer hold out, she came up for air. She heard as the king frantically ordered his men to search every inch of the castle and grounds. Cinderella waited patiently for the men to clear out. She kept her eyes on the clearing wishing she had wings to fly high above in the sky.

A lone guard walked to the water's edge. He looked into the lake as if he knew Cinderella was hiding in the dark liquid. Cinderella knew she was trapped. It was just a matter of seconds before she would have to resurface and when she did, the guard would see her. Cinderella held out her hands and spoke silently into the night. "Out of the water and into the land." The guard came closer to the lake - something was moving within. He placed one foot into the lake and then the other. He slowly made his way further towards the center. He saw the ripples widen as he ventured on.

"Come out, my lady. I know you are here in the water." He reached into the ripples prepared to pull out a woman, but when he searched for her body he realized she was not there. He began to walk backwards, all thoughts of the mysterious woman vanishing from his thoughts. Fish began to leap over his head. He tried to swat at them, but they began to multiply by the dozens. He turned away from the lake and lunged for the shore. He tripped over his own feet and fell upon a bed of frogs. He flung the frogs off his hands as he crawled on the grass. A voice yelled out to him. He turned in shock as rows of fish lined the lake, bellies flapping. "They are breathing! Why are they not dying?" The guard tried to stand, but his feet slipped on all the frogs. Another guard rushed over and helped him to flee.

Cinderella saw her moment. She jumped out of the water sprinting for the forest. She looked back at the lake before exiting the castle grounds. "Out of the land and back to the waters". She watched as the water creatures instantaneously scurried back into the lake.

"There she is! Grab her!"

Cinderella saw a guard pointing at her. She bolted for the forest, but lost her footing tripping over a tree root. Her slipper was caught between the roots. Three guards were charging for her gaining speed. She touched her ankle. "Out of the root". Her foot was released, but the glass slipper stayed lodged in between the twisted root. She raced to her horse calling for him. Faithfully, her steed was by her side in an instant and she climbed on his back. Her dress torn; her hair and body wet. She looked back at the men chasing her before ordering her faithful friend to take her away deep into the forest. "Run, my pet, run! Do not let them catch us!" The horse ran with an uncommon speed racing his mistress to the safety of her magical tree. The guards tried to follow the horse's path, but were mystified when he left no marks in the ground for them to follow. They stopped in bewilderment. The lady had vanished without a trace.

The king was violent and cursed at his guards for allowing the lady to escape his castle.

"She was but a girl! No older than eighteen and she escaped you!" The guards dropped to their knees, begging for forgiveness. "I should have your heads for this! That maiden was to be my queen!"

Marguerite gasped at the news. She had been replaced by a faceless lady no one could remember. She returned to the castle gate with her mother. "He wants that girl! He will only marry her!" she cried.

Lady Tremaine ordered their carriage. "Come, my daughter. All is not lost. If that girl does not want to be found, then the king will be back to search for a queen. He will allow this hunt to continue but a day. Once it settles, and the king admits defeat, he will come to us seeking your hand in marriage. We must be patient and wait."

The guests from the ball cleared out at the news of the king's dismay. All the maidens returned to their homes in defeat. The king paced his castle halls anxious to hear any news on the whereabouts of the mysterious lady. He summoned his trusted footman. "Why can I not recall her features?" The king placed his head against the window, staring into a void of emptiness. "I was just with her, yet her face holds no memory."

"Your Majesty…could it just be you were so mesmerized by her presence that you cannot recall her details?"

The king pondered over the possibility. "It is possible, but I feel it's more than that."

"Perhaps an enchantment, Your Majesty?"

The king's top guard approached holding an object in his hand. "My King, she fled on a gray horse. I was not able to keep up on foot, but I was able to retrieve her glass slipper."

The king was pleased with his guard. "You've done well. I knew I could count on you."

He took the glass slipper holding it up to the candles. "Make an announcement to all the maidens in the land. The lady whose foot can match this tiny slipper shall be my queen." He turned to his footman. "Tomorrow, Norman, at morning's first light you will go to all the homes of all the maidens in my kingdom and try this slipper on every maiden. You will collect the woman who fits this slipper and bring her to me without delay. I shall marry her immediately, putting an end to this mystery."

Cinderella rode through the forest. Cold due to her wet clothes and exhausted by the ordeal she had fled to escape. "He was horrid, my pet, and so forceful. I felt as if he meant to do me harm though I cannot explain why." The horse traveled to the hazel tree bringing his mistress safely home. Cinderella noticed her dress was no longer silver, but black and her glass slipper had turned back to a leaf.

The ivy around her neck was once again just a vine. She walked to the tree, kneeling before it. "Mother, what happened? The king…he was overcome by a frenzy. He scared me Mother."

The tree stroked Cinderella's raven hair, comforting her. "You have witnessed man's true desire…to own a woman."

"I do not want to be owned! I want to be my own mistress."

"And so you are my daughter for you are a princess of magic."

Cinderella shook her head in confusion. "But you wanted me to go. You wanted me to be the queen."

"I did and I still do, my daughter, but not to be ruled by a king. When the king discovers you are The Lady Raven, he will marry you, but the marriage will be short lived. The king is dying. He does not know of his fate, but I have seen it. His heart is failing, and it will not beat much longer."

"I cannot be his bride! I cannot surrender to his suffocating control."

"You will not have to, my daughter. On your wedding night, the king will attempt lay with you, but you will not have to surrender yourself to him. His heart will stop before he can have the pleasure of having you. Once he is dead, you will tell the guards he died consummating the marriage. You will be declared the sole ruler of this kingdom and free from all the chains which have imprisoned you since you came to this land."

Cinderella wrapped her arms around her cold body. "What if you are wrong, mother? What if his heart does not stop and I'm forced into another life of servitude?"

"It will stop, my daughter, for I sent your raven to the castle on the eve of the ball. He carried a vile of poison and dropped it into the king's goblet."

Cinderella wept thinking of her beloved bird. "I miss him so."

The tree shook its branches presenting Cinderella with a black cape to warm her from the bitter cold.

"He is still with you, my daughter. He lives inside of your heart and can never be separated from you."

Cinderella lay underneath the hazel tree with her wolf still in horse form by her side and her mother's branches shielding her from the night. She allowed herself to drift into a deep sleep. Her mind escaped the pain, hurt, and abuse her heart had been carrying since her ravens sacrifice. She dreamed of a life without chains, a life with her raven high above the clouds in which she could soar through the sky.

Cinderella returned to the castle at morning's first light. She was not surprised to find her stepsisters awake, creating a commotion. "The king's footman is on his way! He is almost here! Fetch the beast and tell her to prepare your hair!" Lady Tremaine looked out the windows, eyeing the carriage that was approaching on the horizon. Marguerite rang her bell screaming for her stepsister. Cinderella took one last look around her cellar. If she were to become queen this would be her last moment inside the prison she knew as home. Cinderella entered her stepsister's chamber ready to do her bidding for the last time.

"Hurry you worthless beast! I will not be presented to the king with my hair in tangles!" Cinderella mechanically picked up the comb untangling Marguerite's hair.

"What about us? We have just as much of a chance fitting that slipper as Marguerite!"

Anastasia stood before her mother hands on her hips.

"Maybe so, my daughter." She looked at her twins' feet. "You do have smaller feet than Marguerite."

"What? Mother what are you saying? That slipper is meant to be mine!" insisted Marguerite.

Lady Tremaine picked up Marguerite's foot noticing how uncommonly large it was. "Your feet are too big. That slipper is rumored to be small. It will be impossible for your foot to fit into the glass slipper." She dropped her daughter's foot, returning to her twins. "Your feet hold a better chance if it weren't for your large round heels."

"I'll make my foot fit! I'll jam in my toes and no one will notice."

Lady Tremaine turned to Marguerite eyes wide. "What did you say?"

"My toes…I'll jam them in. I'll make that slipper fit."

"That's it." Lady Tremaine left her daughters returning with a knife.

"Mother? Why do you have a knife?" Marguerite stared at the sharp object in her mother's hand.

"You said you would make your toes fit."

"I did." Marguerite's voice cracked as she answered her mother.

"Yes and the only way to make your toes fit is not to have toes."

Marguerite jumped out of her chair hiding behind Cinderella.

"Mother! No! You can't!"

Lady Tremaine moved closer to her daughter. "Come now child. They are only toes. Think about the reward! To be queen of the entire kingdom! All will love and obey you."

Cinderella became scared for her stepsister. Surely her stepmother couldn't be serious.

"No Mother! I can't!"

"DON'T YOU TELL ME NO, CHILD! Think of all I have sacrificed to get you here. All the bloodshed and loss I have endured for you to be queen! You will do this!" Lady Tremaine called for her twins. "Girls...hold your sister down." Anastasia and Drusilla grabbed their sister throwing her on the ground.

"No Mother! No! Please! Do not do this! I am begging you!"

Cinderella cupped her mouth with her hands, too terrified to witness her stepmother's insanity. She knew she must help her stepsister, but what could she say that wouldn't provoke her stepmother further into her cruel delusion?

"Stepmother? What of the blood?"

Lady Tremaine faced Cinderella. "Blood?"

"Yes...the blood. Her foot will be bloody and the king's hand will surely notice her toes are missing."

Lady Tremaine thought before continuing. "We shall cover her foot in soot, hiding the blood, then wrap it in black satin. The footman will take it as a stocking giving us enough time to fit the slipper." Lady Tremaine got to her knees picking up Marguerite's foot. Marguerite tried to flee from her sister's grasp, but they pinned her forcefully to the ground. Marguerite watched her mother pinch her big toe between her fingers.

"Please Mother! I am begging you! Please do not do this."

Lady Tremaine paid no attention to her daughter's pleas as she began to sever the first toe. Screams filled the castle as Lady Tremaine cut off the second. Marguerite tried to fight off her sisters, but their hold was too strong. Marguerite felt the blood drain from her head, her vision fading into black. All Marguerite could do was scream. She willed her cries to flood the room hoping her anguish would snap her mother out of her crazed state, but Lady Tremaine was not distracted from her task. Thoughts of power, reward, and success overrode her own daughter's turmoil.

She proceeded with the third toe, blocking out Marguerite's cry of pain. Overcome by the unmeasurable torture, Marguerite's head hit the stone floor and she blacked out into unconsciousness. Lady Tremaine threw her daughter's toes into the fire before severing the last remaining two.

"There. All done." announced Lady Tremaine. "Cinderella, collect the soot." Cinderella did not move. She would not take part in this horror. "Did you not hear me you dumb girl? I said get me some soot!"

Again, Cinderella remained still. Lady Tremaine stood up, back handing Cinderella in the face. "You will regret this girl." She walked to the fireplace collecting hot ash. Cinderella realized her stepsister would bleed out if the wound was not cauterized.

"Wait! You need to put her foot in the fire first to stop the blood from bleeding her out."

"Ah…clever girl. Take her to the fire then and be of some use!"

Cinderella dragged her stepsister's unconscious body to the fire thankful she was not awake to feel the pain that was yet to come. She carefully burned the stump with a hot coal sealing the wound. The open flesh meshed together forming angry looking nubs.

"Now cover it with soot." Cinderella backed away not willing to proceed with her stepmother's evil plan. "You blasted girl! I will see you fed to the swines for your stubbornness! Anastasia, cover your sister's foot. Drusilla, fetch me some satin." The girls did as they were told never feeling an ounce of shame for the cruelty they bestowed on their older sister.

Lady Tremaine looked out the window. "They are here." She slapped Marguerite hard across the face ordering her to wake up. "Awake you ungrateful girl!"

Marguerite stirred, slowly awakening from her nightmare. She sat up thankful that the hellish dream was over, but her relief was short lived. A deep festering pain was rose up her leg. She moaned in agony before looking down at her mangled foot. She released a horrific cry breaking off her own fingernails as she dug her hands into the floor. "What have you done to me, Mother?"

Lady Tremaine stared at her daughter with disgust in her eyes. "That's enough! Don't make this act be in vain! Pull yourself together!"

"You mangled me! You made me a cripple for your own greedy needs!"

Lady Tremaine slapped Marguerite once more. "You do not deserve to be queen! You are unfit to rule a kingdom! Look at the opportunity I have given you! Your foot will now fit that slipper sealing your success and all you can concentrate on is your missing toes? I will cut the toes off my own and sew them on to your foot once you are queen. I did this for you! Now get up!"

Marguerite did not move. She wrapped her arms around her chest, rocking back and forth in pain. The twins forcefully lifted Marguerite to the chair. "Do not touch me. You are no sisters of mine. You helped mother. You did this to me."

"Enough with your self-pity, Sister. Mother did this for you." Anastasia placed her hands on her hips, disgusted with her older sister's lack of commitment. "You always were a baby, weren't you Sister?" added Drusilla.

Marguerite shook her head. She couldn't believe her own sisters would be able to inflict such cruelty upon her. Lady Tremaine gripped Marguerite by her shoulder, lifting her chin with her long finger. "I will send the footman up to your room. When he enters, smile and act as if nothing is amiss. Do you understand me girl? If you don't, I will have your other toes."

Marguerite trembled with pain. She knew she would have to play the role that her mother has set in motion. "Yes, Mother."

"Cinderella, send our guest up."

Cinderella crossed her arms, hugging herself as she walked down the staircase. She wanted to run out the door, past the footman, past the garden, and deep into the forest to never return. But she knew Marguerite needed her. She believed her stepmother's words and couldn't leave thinking Marguerite might suffer further by the treacherous hands of her stepmother. Cinderella had to stay by her stepsister's side. No one deserves that kind of abuse. Not even cruel and wicked Marguerite.

Cinderella welcomed the footman into the castle. "The ladies of the house are upstairs."

"Very good, madame." He reached for his parchment reading the royal decree concerning the fitting of the glass slipper.

Cinderella stared at the floor as the footman presented the glass slipper, resting carefully on a velvet pillow. Cinderella detested that slipper. She wanted to smash it into a thousand pieces ending the insanity it had caused. "Follow me, sir. I will take you to my ladies." Cinderella led him up the winding staircase and into Marguerite's room. Her stepmother was standing by Marguerite's side, her hand still resting on her shoulder.

"Good day madame. I have come to fit each maiden of the house with the royal glass slipper. Whomever fits into this delicate slipper shall be queen this very day." The footman walked over to Marguerite, her sisters standing behind her. "I take it you will be first to try on the slipper?" Marguerite smiled a weak smile, all she could muster in her pain.

The footman bent down lifting Marguerite's bandaged foot. He gently placed the foot into the slipper, a perfect fit. "My word! It's a fit! My dear, you shall be queen!"

Lady Tremaine cried out in laughter. "Of course it would be my daughter Marguerite! She is the king's true love and future queen."

Cinderella's eyes stayed focused on the slipper, drops of blood filling the sides. The footman extended his hand to the winner. "Come, my dear. Your carriage awaits." Marguerite stood, losing her balance as she applied pressure on her injury.

"Are you alright madame?"

Marguerite tried to reply, but her words caught in her throat. Her eyes began to tear with pain. The footman looked over at the mother knowing something was wrong.

"What is the matter with her?"

Lady Tremaine cast her hand in the air, waving it around. "She is just in shock at the excitement of the moment, sir. She will be fine once she is at the castle."

The footman did not believe Lady Tremaine and dropped Marguerite's hand. "Walk to me madame." he said to Marguerite.

"This is absurd! There was no decree to perform party tricks just to try on the slipper!"

The footman ignored Lady Tremaine and again commanded Marguerite to walk forward.

Marguerite took one step before crying out in pain, collapsing to the floor. The footman went to her side lifting up her leg. Blood spilled out of the slipper. "What is the meaning of this?" He removed the slipper undressing Marguerite's foot. He jumped up in shock by the display before him. "You cut off your own daughter's toes so she would fit into the slipper!"

Lady Tremaine tried to explain. She walked over to her daughter giving some excuse for her recent injury, but the footman called for the royal guards. "Not only is this a wicked and cruel thing to do to one's daughter, but you also have committed treason against the king by attempting to trick him! You will be sentenced for this my lady!" He turned to the twins, their faces smeared with guilt. "Did you two have a part in this?"

They shook their heads no, too ashamed and scared to admit their guilt.

"Hold out your hands."

The guards grabbed the girls' hands, revealing blood under their nails. "Away with them! Let them join their mother in the dungeon." He faced Marguerite, anger in his eyes.

"What to do with you? You obviously played a role in this deception. You lost your toes, but you will not go unjudged. You have already received your punishment, but you will not go free from this crime. Take her to the castle and let her be judged by the king."

Cinderella watched as her stepmother and stepsisters were dragged away by the guards. She knew that would be the last time she ever saw those horrid women and a sense of freedom came over her.

"And you servant…what say you about this?"

Cinderella looked at the ground.

"I did not hurt my stepsister or take part in the mangling. I did burn her wounds with hot coal to prevent her from bleeding out, but that was all."

The footman grabbed Cinderella's hands seeing burn marks from the coal. "You speak the truth, but something is odd. You say those ladies were your stepsisters?" Cinderella nodded. "Why would you be a servant in your own home?" Cinderella remained silent, upset that she revealed too much already.

"Let me see your feet." Cinderella lifted her dress exposing her bare feet. "They are so small…so tiny." He reached for the slipper holding it before Cinderella. "Try it on."

Cinderella denied the footman's request. "Madame, I said try on the slipper."

"I do not wish to try it on."

The footman moved back amazed by such a response. "It is not a request, it is an order. Try on the slipper." Two guards came towards Cinderella, they would use force if she denied again. She placed her hand on the mantel for balance as her foot slipped inside the slipper. "I knew it would be a fit." he whispered.

Cinderella closed her eyes knowing she would be whisked away to the castle, to be the queen of a king whom she did not love. "Come, Madame. Your king awaits." He held out his hand and Cinderella reluctantly accepted. Her heart was broken, her spirit crushed and despite her mother's assurances, her dreams of freedom died inside her as she walked with the footman leaving the hall.

They made their way to the royal carriage where Cinderella took one last glance at the castle which had been her home for so many years. "Please, I have to go into the forest before we depart."

"That is not possible, my lady. You might escape a second time and the king would surely have my head."

"Please. Your guards can accompany me. They can chain me if you wish, but I need to collect my horse. I cannot leave without him."

The footman agreed ordering his guards to chain Cinderella to them. "You may retrieve your horse." The guards chained her wrists, clenching the end.

"My thanks sir."

Cinderella led the guards through the forest to the hazel tree where the gray horse was waiting underneath. "I need to grab two things from the tree, then I am ready."

The guard tugged on her chain reminding her she was on a short leash. Cinderella reached inside the tree, feeling the raven's small coffin.

"You came for a horse and a box?" asked the guard.

Cinderella turned to the guard, "And a twig." She solemnly broke a twig, one glass leaf attached. Cinderella whispered to her mother's tree. "Be at peace now for I must leave. I will replant the hazel branch and call your spirit forth once again." Cinderella turned to the guards. "I am ready."

Another guard took hold of the horse's mane and walked it back to the carriage. "Come now. You have your horse and your odd little box. It's time we departed. No more delays." he said dragging her away from the forest.

Cinderella climbed into the carriage keeping the wooden coffin safely in her arms. They rode in silence, Cinderella felt anxious. She wished her horse was a wolf again and her raven alive flying amongst the sky.

A Queen Is Crowned

Cinderella entered the king's throne bare foot, alone, and defeated. The king stood up the moment he saw his lady's face. "It is you! My Lady of the House of Raven." Cinderella curtsied to her future husband. He grabbed her forcefully, embracing her limp body and suffocating her with a kiss. "We shall be married immediately." He whispered in her ear.

"As you wish, my king."

The king ordered for the priest before realizing his bride was dressed in rags. "Where is your gown? Where are your shoes?"

Cinderella shrugged. "This is my gown, my king."

"This will never do! I will send for a proper gown! One meant for a queen." He turned to his footman. "Gather the most exquisite white gown in my kingdom and a glass slipper to match its twin."

Cinderella stopped the king. "Not white, your majesty but black with a glass pendent for a bridal necklace." Cinderella held out one of her mother's glass leaves.

The king laughed at his new bride's request. "A black wedding gown? That is unheard of. One would think my queen is attending a funeral and not her own wedding."

"My only wish is to be married to my King in a black wedding gown."

The king rubbed his chin in astonishment. "You truly are the most unique woman I have ever known. Very well. A black wedding dress to match your black hair."

Cinderella curtsied in thanks. "May I wait in my chamber before the gown arrives?"

The king thought before answering. "Very well, but only if you are securely locked inside and my guards await behind the door."

"That will suit me fine, my King."

Cinderella followed the king through the grand castle. Gold trim lined the ceiling and majestic crystal chandeliers hung before her. It was truly the most impressive castle she had ever seen. The king opened her chamber door revealing a room the size of a small house. Gold tapestries hung above her magnificent canopy bed and everything was touched with gold. Even the fireplace was lined with a gold ornate trim. She rubbed her hand over the gold bedspread. She felt out of place and she longed for the small quarters of her cellar.

"I shall send your gown up when it arrives. Your handmaidens will bath and dress you before our wedding."

"Thank you, my King, I shall be waiting."

The king, uninvited, kissed her once again smothering her mouth. She detested his taste and hated his scent. Her nostrils flared with disgust. "So shall I, my queen." He said releasing his grip.

Cinderella remained composed until the door shut, locking from the outside.

She threw herself on the bed, drowning in tears. "My love, I wish you were alive and here with me now. I feel more alone than I ever have in all my years. I am but a shadow of my former self without you, my love." Cinderella held her bird inside his wooden box allowing sleep to take her to a better place in the world of dreams.

She awoke to the door being unlocked. Seven handmaidens entered, holding the gown as if it were a person suspended in air. A bath was prepared. Cinderella had forgotten the touch of warm water. She lay still allowing the warm water to baptize her, making her anew. Her hair was combed and was to be left down by the order of the king. She preferred it down and was grateful to feel it caress her back. She stood, arms raised as the handmaidens slipped the magnificent gown over her head. It fit her body like a glove and she welcomed the feel of cool silk against her skin. A matching glass slipper arrived with another handmaiden. It mirrored her own to perfection and she placed her feet into the slippers feeling rejuvenated. She walked to the mirror admiring her reflection. The footman arrived bewitched by Cinderella's beauty.

"My lady, you are breathtaking. The king shall be pleased."

Cinderella walked to the footman staring deep into his eyes. "I am not your lady. I am The Lady Raven. Hair as black as night, eyes as blue as the sea, and skin as clear as glass."

The footman bowed, impressed by Cinderella's change in demeanor. She confidently entered the throne room with her head held high. All who saw her bowed instantly at the sight of her beauty. The king himself fell speechless as he gazed upon his bride. Cinderella held out her hand to the king.

"Let us begin, my King."

The King accepted her hand kissing it as he gazed into the face of the woman who bewitched him. The ceremony was speedy, lasting only minutes. The King wanted it to be over before it could begin as he was anxious to claim his prize. Cinderella spoke her vows with a stoic air feeling nothing for the man she promised them for. There was to be no ball and no party following the ceremony. The king was too eager to make his bride his own. They were to depart immediately for her chamber. A golden crown was placed on Cinderella's head, symbolising her royalty. The king was satisfied by his choice.

He walked Cinderella to the outside balcony where a sea of faces stretched out before them. The entire kingdom awaited on the castle grounds eager and curious to meet their new queen. The king presented his bride to his subjects.

"My kingdom, I present to you your new queen! Serve her well for her beauty holds no equal!"

Cinderella looked into the faces of her subjects. Hundreds were cheering the welcome of their new queen. "I am The Lady Raven, your queen. On my life I promise to rule well and serve my kingdom justly and with truth.

As I am yours, you are also mine! I shall love, protect, and serve you all the days of my life."

The crowd roared with praise as they loved her already. The king smiled with pride at his new bride. "Very well spoken my wife. Come…we will have a lifetime to rule. I am in need of your exclusive company."

He raced Cinderella to her chambers locking the door behind him. Proof would be required, so Cinderella knew she would have to pretend to consummate the marriage. She was grateful to be alone with her husband unseen behind a locked door. The king rushed to her stripping off her gown. He grabbed her body as if he were a wolf hungry for flesh. She tried not to flinch as he kissed her skin making his way to her navel. She imagined her raven flying in the sky. She wanted to be a bird and to be able to fly through the window and into the crowd waiting below.

She was lifted and thrown onto the bed. The king was not kind, he was not gentle, and his intentions were something raw and savage. He pulled on her hair as he climbed on top of her back. He began to strip off his own clothes, panting like an animal. Cinderella kept thinking of her mother's words. "His heart will fail…his heart will fail". I will not be taken this day. Soon his heart will fail. The thoughts traveled through her head as he clawed at her back, tearing her flesh. She waited, trying not to lash out in anger. She waited as the king told her that she would be his and only his – forever. His hands flipped her over pushing her shoulders into the mattress.

He held her down as he told her they would soon be one. "This time will not be for you, my wife, but for me. I will take you hard and take all of you. On this day, I am claiming you for my own. Your mind, your body, and your soul. It shall all belong to me until death does part us."

She closed her eyes fearing her mother had lied. She would not live a life as a slave. She would rather die than spend one more day with this monster. She accepted her mother's lie and made a promise to end her own life when the moon arose in the night sky. Cinderella braced herself for the consummation praying it would be quick. But as she closed her eyes everything stopped. The king collapsed on her body, his breathing coming to an end. She called out to him, but he did not move. She pushed his shoulders away, but he did not respond. She slid out from underneath him turning him on his back.

"My King? My King!" She placed her head next to his heart…nothing. She placed her two fingers on his neck…no pulse. She fell on her heels, grateful her mother spoke the truth and she was ashamed to have distrusted her. Quickly, she grabbed a robe from the wardrobe and carefully planned her next move. She would need proof of their time together. She took the branch from her mother's tree and scratched her arm with it. "Where there is no blood let this branch bring forth a puddle of deception." She placed the branch on the bed and bit her lip as her spell worked its magic. Blood poured forth from the branch creating a tiny puddle on the sheets. She sighed in relief, knowing her life would be secure and her place as queen untouchable. She returned her branch to the dresser and cried out in horror.

"Help! Someone help! The king is not moving!" She unlocked the door allowing the guards to rush to their king. They listened for his heart, but there was no sound to be heard. "He just stopped! He just stopped breathing! I don't understand!" Cinderella cupped her face in her hands as false tears of agony fell from her eyes.

The guards noticed the puddle of blood and sent for the royal counsel. Cinderella's handmaidens took her to another part of her chamber fussing over her as the counsel deliberated over the scene before them. "It does indeed look as if he died of heart failure while consummating the marriage." One member of the counsel pondered over the situation. Another walked over and inspected the bed, assuring the others that they did indeed have a moment together. "The evidence is all here. They did become husband and wife sealing their marriage. This is all nothing more than a tragic accident." declared the counsel men.

They went to their queen offering words of sympathy. "It is a tragic event, my Queen, but it was just an act of unfortunate circumstances. The king had worked himself up in these past few days with too much commotion and excitement. It took its toll on the king's heart and now he is gone."

Cinderella arose from her chair wiping pretend tears from her eyes. "I am deeply sorry for your loss of the king, but I promise to reign in his stead as a just and loyal queen to all my subjects." The counsel bowed to their new queen believing her words, they knew Cinderella would serve her kingdom well.

My Love, He Is Again

Months passed. Cinderella did indeed rule in grace and fairness and her subjects adored their new queen. She was loved by all and admired by any who stood in her presence. She did not sentence her stepmother and stepsisters to the dungeon. She found another punishment for them. They were appointed the Royal Swine Herders, sleeping in the servant's quarter by the barn designed especially for them. Her stepmother soon died due to the work being too hard on her pampered body. Her remaining stepsisters found peace living amongst the animals. Soon, they turned from their wicked ways and into hard workers. They had met true humility and lived their life quietly amongst each other. Cinderella offered them an open pass to leave at any time as they were not her slaves, but paid workers. Like all her servants, they had a choice. But in the end, the girls knew they had nowhere else to go and could not find a better life than where they were.

Cinderella kept true to her routine, roaming the night, and venturing into the forest. She was searching for the perfect spot to plant her mother's branch. She missed her tree and wanted desperately to hear her mother's spirit once again. Her faithful horse was kept in the royal stable.

She rode him daily enjoying their time together, but she missed his form as a wolf. She would sit with her steed under an apple tree, much like the one that she had cherished in Munich. Together, they would sit in silence, sharing an apple with her thoughts drifting back to the memory of her beloved raven. "I miss my love. He was the only true friend I have ever known. I long for the days when it was just us again, walking amongst the stars with magic in the air." She stroked her horse's face placing her own against his velvet fur. "I am so blessed to have you, my pet. You are my one and only now. Stay with me all your days."

Cinderella awoke that night from a deep sleep hearing her mother's words entering through the window.

"My daughter, it is time to plant your branch."

Cinderella arose from her bed, donning a black dress. She picked up her mother's branch along with her raven's coffin. She ventured into the night sky feeling alive. She gathered her horse asking him to accompany her to the forest. They walked together in silence enjoying the darkness which concealed them. She came to a circle of trees where the moonlight streaked through the clouds illuminating the center of the circle.

"This will be our spot my pet." She placed three stones outside the trees. "From my will, protect this sacred spot for a barrier no one can penetrate."

The three stones transformed into magnificent boulders reaching higher than the trees. She caught a mole, hiding under a branch. She took the mole to the sacred boulders. "Go inside little one." The mole tried to go through the boulders, but he was unable to do so. He tried to go around, but the three boulders seemed endless and did not allow even an inch of space through which to enter. Cinderella was satisfied. Her spell had worked. "Come, my pet. Let us enter and make new magic." She walked into the space through the boulders. Her body moved through them as if it were air, her horse following behind.

She placed her raven beside her, opening the coffin. She plucked a feather from his wing and kissed her bird on the head. "My pet, may I collect a strand of hair from your gorgeous mane?" The horse willingly lowered his head for his queen. She took only a single strand and kneeled in the moonlight placing her raven beside her. She began to dig a hole with her hands. She removed the glass leaf from the branch tying it to a piece of ivy making a necklace. She placed the necklace around her neck and buried her mother's branch. This time she did not add the glass, but one raven feather and a single strand of horse hair.

She looked to the moon and extended her arms, tears streaking her cheeks. "What once I had, but then I lost. What once was found, but then taken. I ask for all to be as it was. Return to me this very night! Transform the love within a feather, into the form of my mother and bring her spirit forth to grow again!"

The ground shifted revealing a branch. Cinderella chanted her spell over and over until the branch formed a body and grew more branches. Cinderella called for the tree to grow until it was the size and form of a woman.

Unlike the first time, this tree had no glass leaves, but black feathers which extended out into the night. The tree shook, an ebony glitter falling from its feathered wings like star dust from the sky. Cinderella felt her wolf's head once again resting on her lap. "My pet! You are back to your gorgeous self again." The wolf licked her hand grateful to be in his true form. Her mother's words spoke from the tree.

"My darling daughter, your powers have grown so. Not only are you a royal queen, but a truly talented witch."

"I have missed you mother."

"And I have missed you, my lovely daughter."

Cinderella admired her mother's new leaves. She stroked the feathers longing for her raven. She reached for the coffin but cried at the empty box. "This wasn't supposed to happen...he was supposed to return to me." She frantically looked around the ground, searching for his body. "I don't understand. It should have worked. Why didn't it work?"

Her mother wiped Cinderella's tears with a feather. "It did work, my daughter." The tree spread its feathers into the sky opening a passage from inside the tree. Cinderella watched in amazement as a man walked forth from the branches.

"But...who is this? Where is my raven?"

The man kneeled beside Cinderella. His hair black as coal, his eyes dark as midnight without a moon. His smile was kind, so familiar and loving. He stroked Cinderella's face whispering into her ear. "My princess, do you not recognize your love?"

Cinderella lunged into his arms crying as she clung to her raven's new form. "My love, is it really you?"

"Yes, my princess. You have brought me back. I am as I once was."

Cinderella faced her love examining his new features. "But you were my raven and now you are human. I don't understand."

He smiled, rubbing his nose against hers. "I was your raven, but before I came to you that day by your mother's grave I was a man. I have returned to my true form."

Cinderella smiled, overcome by the emotion of love. "I do not care what form you take for you are my love and always will be." She kissed his cheek never wanting to leave their place under the feather tree.

"And you have always been my princess, my love, since the moment I saw you I have been lost to you." He winked at Cinderella. "I suppose now you are my queen."

She laughed, shaking her head. "Oh no, my love, we are equal. I may be your queen, but only if you will be my king."

He traced his thumb over her lips. "I will be anything you want me to be." He kissed her. A soft, true love's kiss…a kiss which could stop time and made their love immortal.

Epilogue

Cinderella sat in her chair rocking the sleeping infant in her arms. She was deeply in love with her baby, Gabriella. Her hair was as black as ravens' wings, her eyes dark as onyx, and her lips as red as roses. She sang to Gabriella a song of ever after and true love. "One day, my sweet daughter, you shall be a lady...a lady of magic. I shall teach you how to command the night sky, summon the earth, and take night creatures as your faithful companions." Gabriella cooed, staring into her mother's eyes. "I shall love and keep you safe until my dying day and beyond that, my beautiful daughter." Gabriella reached for her mother's leaf pendant and she touched the glass releasing sparkles over Gabriella's delicate face. "One day, you will don this pendant, my little love, and all the powers it holds."

A guard knocked on the chamber door. "My Queen, your presence is requested in the throne room. There is a situation that needs your urgent attention." Cinderella called for her loyal wet nurse. "Stay with her. I shall return shortly." The nurse smiled, loving the baby princess as if she were her own. Cinderella kissed her baby before exiting her chamber. Cinderella entered the grand throne room with her faithful wolf by her side. She took her place on the throne, stroking her gray pet. "Councilman, what is this dire situation that requires my immediate attention?"

"Your Majesty, there has been a disturbance in the forest."

"What sort of disturbance?"

The head councilman took a step closer. "There are rumors that a witch has taken refuge in the deepest part of the forest. The villagers saw her roaming the night. She is searching for humans to sacrifice for her beast that resides with her."

Cinderella thought, her mind mentally venturing into the forest. In all her years as queen, she had never seen another witch in the forest. Surely if there was another woman of power Cinderella would have sensed her presence. "I am not aware of a dark presence in the forest. I have never sensed such a woman. Are you sure it is our forest which she occupies?"

"Yes, my Queen. She is said to be a beautiful witch with a magic mirror."

Cinderella leaned in her seat, motioning for the councilman to come closer. "A magic mirror you say?"

"Yes, my queen."

"Where is the king? My husband, Corvus?"

"He has gone into the forest to search for the witch."

Cinderella jumped to her feet, her wolf by her side. "Collect my horse. I will depart immediately." Cinderella ran to the stables mounting her horse, rejecting any assistance from her guards to accompany her. "Thank you for your loyalty, but I require your presence here at the castle. Protect the princess. Stay with her and let no one enter or exit the castle until my return."

"My Queen, you should not venture into the forest alone! It is unsafe!"

Cinderella smiled at her trusted knight. He was loyal to her as all her knights and guards were and they would willingly give their life to protect her. Not purely out of duty, but out of love. "I do not need protection brave knight. My daughter, your princess, is the one who needs to be protected. I shall return soon so do not fear for me. I travel with my wolf and with the powers of the earth."

Cinderella rode off into the forest, the castle drawbridge closing up behind her. The forest was eerily quiet. She could sense a disturbance in the trees. "Something is indeed here, my pet. The creatures are too quiet. The wind does not blow through the leaves." Cinderella traveled deep into the forest where dead animals lined a path leading up to a hut made from an old tree stump. Cinderella dismounted her horse placing her hands on a dead fox. Its heart had been carefully removed. "Show me the evil which took your heart." whispered Cinderella. A vision of a cloaked figure stood before her, a shadow of recent events. The cloaked figure pointed to the fox, green mist entering the fox's body. He dropped to the ground falling on his back. The cloaked figure took its long nail and sliced opened the fox removing its beating heart. The figure placed the heart into a glass jar and walked out of view into the forest.

Cinderella was disturbed by the vision. She knew this was dark magic. "This sorcerer has evil intentions, my pet.

She means harm to the forest animals and harm to this kingdom. If she is collecting beating hearts from animals, she is conjuring a dark plan for the people of my kingdom. It will just be a matter of time before she is also collecting human hearts." She looked at her wolf, disturbed by her findings. "We must visit my mother. Maybe she has heard whispers of what this sorcerer is planning." They rode back to her hazel tree; her mother's branches spread wide waiting for Cinderella.

"My daughter, you have discovered the evil which roams the forest."

"Mother, who is the sorcerer that means this land harm?"

"She comes from another kingdom where her rule has come to an end. She is looking to claim this land as her own. You and your family are in grave danger, my daughter. She is very powerful, more powerful than any magic you have come against. This is dark, evil magic which requires blood sacrifices."

"My counsel said she is rumored to have a magic mirror. Mother, is that from one of your glass leaves?"

"Yes, my daughter."

Cinderella touched her leaf pendant terror rising inside her. "This is not your magic pendant, is it?"

"No, it is not. While you were asleep, the sorceress crept into your room and switched the pendants while you were in a deep sleep. She is extremely powerful and she transformed herself into an owl casting a sleep like death upon you and Corvus. You only awoke because of the true love you and Corvus share."

"What shall I do? How do I retrieve the pendant?"

"You cannot. Corvus was just here. He had discovered the sorcerer's latest victim, the young daughter of a hunter. Her heart was cut out. He has gone back to the glass tree to burn it."

"No! It's too dangerous! I must go after him!"

"Be careful my daughter. I cannot protect you from this evil. She is more powerful than I."

Cinderella raced back to her horse. "I shall return shortly mother."

"Wait!"

But Cinderella did not stop to listen to her mother. She raced fast into the forest, her steed kicking up the earth as they rode to the glass tree. Thoughts of her beloved alone and in danger crippled her. She would not lose him again.

She came upon the glass tree. The leaves were dead of their sparkle with no magic living inside. She saw Corvus's horse near the tree. Terror gripped her as she dismounted her horse. "He is here, my wolf. Be careful. I fear we are not alone."

Cinderella walked up to the glass tree. Its branches were closed and she broke off a branch.

"Corvus! Corvus! Where are you my love?" She listened for a response, but none was to be heard. Her hands trembled as she feared the worst.

She commanded the tree to open its branches, but it would not obey her request. "Open for me!" The tree stood still, its limbs closed tight. "I am The Lady Raven, Queen of Magic in this land and I command you to open!"

"You are no queen to me, Your Majesty. I have a new queen who commands me."

"What is her name? Who commands you, tree?"

"She is known as Grimhilde, the true queen of magic."

Cinderella did not know of a Grimhilde and she was perplexed as to where this witch came from. "I am the true ruler of this kingdom and of you! You will surrender to me!"

Cinderella held out her arm invoking the powers around her. "By my hands you will open to me! I release Grimhildes hold on you! Open now!"

The tree unwillingly opened its branches. Cinderella noticed two boots dangling from the center. "Corvus!!!" As the tree unfolded, Corvus hung motionless, dangling inside the tree.

Cinderella ran to him, but the tree carried his body further up. "Release him!"

"He is alive, my queen."

Cinderella turned as a cloaked figure stood behind her. "You! Grimhilde, release my husband, your king, or suffer the consequence."

The sorcerer laughed. "You are a fighter. But no, I will not release your precious love."

The wolf came upon the witch snarling his white teeth at her. "How charming, you brought a pet." Grimhilde said amused.

"What do you want?"

The sorcerer walked over to the side of the tree, keeping her distance from Cinderella.

"That is a key question, is it not, my queen? What do I want?"

"Enough riddles! Speak your request!" Cinderella eyed her husband hanging in the tree, his mouth gagged by glass leaves and his arms tangled in branches.

"Ha-ha-ha. You are feisty. Very well. What I want is simple…I want to be queen."

"Never."

"Ah, do not answer so hastily, my dear. For I hold your beloved at my mercy."

Cinderella shuddered. She was helpless to the sorceress's demands.

"You see, I have thought this through very carefully. The king holds no threat to me. If he is without a queen, I would serve him well for a substitute. I am very beautiful and with my beauty and a memory charm your beloved would soon forget all about his true love." Grimhilde removed her cloak revealing her enchanting face. She was indeed beautiful; the most beautiful woman Cinderella had ever seen.

"Then there is the question of your daughter, the little princess. Now, if I were to kill her that would hold a threat to me for two reasons. A man losing both a wife and a child is not as easy to bewitch. My spell on him could backfire causing him harm before I was named queen." Grimhilde walked in a complete circle around the tree.

"Second, if I were to murder the princess, as queen I would be obligated to produce an heir. Seeing that I am barren and unable to perform such a ghastly act against nature, I would be replaced with a queen who could bear the king a child."

Cinderella clenched her fists tight, her wolf growling louder by her side.

"So, as you see, my remaining option is to just eliminate the competition by killing you."

"Try it and see who suffers, witch."

"Exactly my dear. I know I am no match for you. Your powers are too strong. You have grown into a very potent sorceress. I might die trying and that would not benefit me."

"What are you proposing, Grimhilde?"

"That you surrender yourself to me, allow me to cut out your heart, and consume your magic. In return, I will not kill your beloved who is held captive in my tree. As you can plainly see, he is still alive, but struggling for his life. His time is short and if you do not give your heart to me willingly, I will take your true love's heart and eat it in front of you."

Cinderella willed her emotions silent. Her stoic nature had never failed her before, saving her in a past life of abuse and torture. She needed to collect herself to think clearly. There is always a way out, always something one can do to survive. Corvus hung in the tree, squirming for release. He would rather die, his heart consumed by Grimhilde then see Cinderella harmed. Cinderella whispered in her wolf's ear, planting a kiss on his head. She faced Grimhilde ready to sacrifice her own life for her love. "Promise me that neither my husband nor my daughter will ever be harmed."

Corvus began to bite down on the leaves breaking them in his mouth. He spat the glass on the ground calling out to Cinderella. "No! Do not do her bidding! Fight! End my life, but do not surrender yours!"

Cinderella looked at her love as she placed her finger over her mouth. "It is alright, my love. We will always be together." Corvus frantically tried to free himself screaming in terror as Cinderella kneeled before the witch.

"Do not worry, lover." said Grimhilde. "I shall serve you well as your new queen. You will soon forget about your precious wife kneeling before me. All your thoughts will revolve around me and your complete devotion."

"I will kill you if you harm her!"

"Fool! Why do you think you are up there and I am down here? You will never have the opportunity to destroy me."

Cinderella gripped the broken branch chanting silently as Grimhilde walked over to her.

"Out of the death and into the fire. Out of the death and into the fire." The branch began to smoke, hot flames burning inside Cinderella's hand. Grimhilde did not notice Cinderella's magic for she was casting her own. "From life to death, bring me her heart." Grimhilde closed her eyes working her spell.

Cinderella felt a sharp pain enter her chest. She knew time was of the essence. Her wolf jumped into the tree breaking off branches with his powerful jaws. Shards of glass rained down on the sorceress causing her magic to pause. She flung the wolf onto the ground, but he did not stay down. He was up and gnawing at the witch's hands. She called out in pain as he bit through her bones. Corvus jumped out of the tree landing by the wolf's side.

Cinderella saw her opportunity and cast the burning branch into hazel tree. It ignited. Brilliant flames encircling the tree, consuming it in a ring of fire. Cinderella ran to Grimhilde, her heart weak from the magic that was cast upon her. "Corvus! The pendant! Grab the pendant!"

The wolf jumped on top of the witch throwing her to the ground. Corvus reached for the pendant tearing it off her neck. He tossed it to Cinderella as she fastened it around her own. "Into the flames!" cried Cinderella. Grimhilde screamed as her body began to ignite, burning on fire. She quickly transformed into an owl flying off into the sky.

Corvus grabbed Cinderella. "Are you ok? Your heart?"

"Take me to my mother."

Corvus climbed onto his horse placing Cinderella across his lap. "Hold on, my love! Stay with me! Do not go where I cannot follow."

Cinderella clenched her heart feeling her life slip away. She willed her body to go on and willed her heart to keep beating. She was not ready to depart this world. She could not bear the thought of leaving her daughter and husband behind. "My soul will not survive without you and Gabriella to love. If I die before you I will vanish into extinction. I am not ready to go yet."

Corvus hushed his wife as he came to the magical tree. He carried Cinderella to her mother's branches prepared to once again sacrifice himself to save his true love's life. He placed Cinderella in the tree, the feather leaves closing around her. "Take my life! Spare hers! You did it once. Do it again!"

"I cannot. Two of the same sacrifice cannot be made to save one life. It requires another." The wolf came forth bowing to the tree.

"Faithful wolf, I am afraid your life is not significant enough to save our Cinderella." She placed a feather branch over the whimpering wolf. "Please, remain with my daughter for all time. She loves you so. Come here, Corvus."

Corvus knelt before the tree, eyes stained with tears. "You must burn me."

"I cannot. You are her mother. She needs you."

"No, my sweet man, she needs you. I have done all I can for our precious girl in this world and now it is up to you to take care of her. Once I am gone no more evil will be able to find its way to these woods. My magical presence brought that sorceress to this kingdom and it would eventually bring more. The only way to keep Cinderella safe is to burn me. I am the last sacrifice."

Corvus plucked a feather from the tree holding it tight. "Burn bright set aflame to this night." Corvus was surprised to realize the sun had set. He watched as his feather became bright with fire illuminating the night sky.

"Throw the fire into my branches. The flames will not harm Cinderella. When I am burned and reduced to ashes, Cinderella will awaken."

"Goodbye, my lady."

"Goodbye, sweet friend. I know that you will always stay with my daughter."

Corvus threw the feather into the tree sitting on his heels as it burned into the ground.

The wolf stayed by Corvus's side, both praying Cinderella would emerge from the smoke unharmed and whole. As the smoke cleared, Cinderella did walk forth untouched by the fire. Her hair no longer raven but white as star dust from the death of her mother. Corvus embraced her in his arms, scooping her up as if she was a child.

"It is over my love. It is done."

Cinderella nestled her head into his shoulders. "I know, my love, I know…"